Blairsville Junior High School

By James Cloyd Bowman

MIKE FINK

Snapping Turtle of the O-hi-o-o
Snag of the Massassip

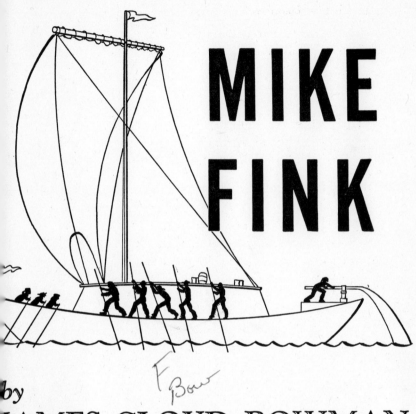

MIKE
FINK

by
JAMES CLOYD BOWMAN

illustrated by
LEONARD EVERETT FISHER

LITTLE, BROWN and COMPANY
Boston · Toronto

Published simultaneously in Canada
by Little, Brown & Company (Canada) Limited

PRINTED IN THE UNITED STATES OF AMERICA

T O

Herman Charles

and

Herman W.

Contents

MIKE FINK

1. Alone on the Wilderness Trail

Alone on the wilderness trail, Mike Fink moved nimble as a wild wolf, furtive as a shadow, sly as a fox. His jet-black hair reached to his shoulders; his face was covered with a silky sheen of down, soft as the breast of a wildfowl, and was tanned brown as a berry. He stood straight as a bean pole, and was rugged as an ox.

Young Mike was a member of the Government Scout Troop, stationed at Fort Pitt. He was helping his outfit drive the treacherous Indians out of the territory, thus opening the Wilderness for the white settlers. His troop had outwitted the Indians at their own game. Mike was now on his way back to Fort Pitt, the western outpost of civilization.

It was four months since Mike had seen a white man. He had been living the life of an Indian, feeding on parched corn and wild meat. He was dressed in buckskin hunting shirt and pantaloons, and shod with Indian moccasins to disguise his tracks. His coonskin cap with its dangling plume was cocked over his left ear. He carried a flintlock rifle and a long hunting knife.

Lately the weather had turned sour, and for days on end there had been nothing but wind and rain, more wind and more rain. Mike had been unable to snare small game. He was hungry. This morning when the sun had come up and the day was clear, he had started along the trail in search of food.

He had not gone far when he came upon fresh signs of deer, and he followed the tracks in the soft ground. Mike never fired his rifle unless it was necessary. He knew if Indians happened to be near and heard the report, he would probably be ambushed.

Mike moved with the utmost caution, slinking from the shelter of one tree to the next. He stopped often to look in every direction and listen. At the end of an hour he sighted a beautiful buck feeding. The deer took a bite of deer moss, threw up its head, ears alert. Then it stepped forward, nipped the top off a maple sprout, and again looked and listened.

Mike sifted powder in the pan of his rifle and tiptoed noiselessly ahead, keeping the next tree between him and the deer. Out of the corner of his eye he saw the quick flicker of a shadow to the right of the deer. He stopped in the shelter of a tree for a clearer view.

A big Indian warrior had also sighted the buck, and was creeping stealthily forward, but from a different direction. The Indian was now within easy firing range, and stopped to prime his rifle.

Quick as a flash Mike drew back his leg, lifted his rifle to his shoulder, and waited. The instant he saw smoke from the Indian's rifle, he crooked his trigger finger. The Indian let out a yell, threw up his hands, and fell upon his face.

Mike reloaded his rifle. He crouched low, waiting to see if the gunfire would bring any curious Indians. When he had satisfied himself that none were near, he went to inspect the warrior. He found him dead, a bullet hole over his heart. He also discovered the Indian's rifle bore the stamp "U. S. A.," and concluded it had been smuggled out of the fort by the traitor Simon Girty and his followers. But now it was certain no warriors lived to attack the fort. The scout troop had made sure of that.

This lone Indian had brought down his last buck. Mike deftly cut away the hindquarters, threw them across his shoulder, and disappeared, silent as a phantom.

When Mike reached Fort Pitt he learned that the news of the frontier's being at last secure against Indians had traveled like wildfire to the tidewater country. Western migration was growing swiftly as the water in the Ohio River during the spring freshet. It was now at flood tide.

Young Mike could scarcely believe his eyes. New cabins were springing up like mushrooms. Small shops of all sorts had already opened their doors along Water Street, facing the Monongahela River. Ephraim Jones's tavern, the Sign of the Catfish, near the ferry landing, was filled with travelers. Chevalier Duboc, a Frenchman of noble birth, was operating a dry goods and grocery store. He traded his wares to trappers and hunters for furs and hides, and to the farmers for grain and tobacco. He was happy, indeed, when a customer brought in a bundle of dried ginseng roots. Duboc kept a great Dane dog, Sultan, and a mischievous monkey, Bijou, to delight the children, old and young.

Judge Breckenridge was just finishing a pretentious house with several rooms and fireplaces, enclosed by a high picket fence, painted blue. His shingle was out. Peter Mowry, a former student at the best European universities, had resigned from the Army Post, and was practicing medicine. Without knowing it, Mike was witnessing the first steps in the building of Pittsburgh.

Throughout the town there was the bustle of excitement. Everyone was talking about the unlimited opportunities to be found in the New West, of the vast stretches of free land and natural resources. The streets were crowded with emigrants headed down the Ohio River, to begin life all over again. They waited, restless and ill at ease, till they could hire passage on some sort of river craft.

Mike talked with the rivermen. Their tales of wild adventure awakened old memories and fired his imagination. He had grown up near Fort Pitt. His uncle, Roving Charley, a trapper and explorer, had been a father to him.

Now, as soon as Mike had satisfied his curiosity over the growing town, he set out to find his Uncle Charley. Finally Ephraim Jones directed him to the last cabin down the river.

Mike found Roving Charley plumb disgusted. "Well, I'll be tarred and feathered if I don't feel like pickin' up my traps and movin' on where the West's still a wilderness!" He struck his coonskin cap on his knee for emphasis. "Why, I can't move out o' my tracks without seein' the nose of some inquisitive neighbor stickin' between the trees. These fellers round here don't understand what liberty is, or they wouldn't be meddlin' with it!"

Mike tried to say something, but Roving Charley was too excited to listen.

"Before this shyster lawyer put up his shingle, there wasn't no dispute honest men couldn't settle with tongue-lashin' or fisticuffs. And before this Army Post medicine feller put out *his* shingle, the only way a man could be rubbed out in this healthy wilderness was with a long rifle; but soon this nanny goat'll have everybody believin' in a hundred different ailments, and gulpin' down vile potions. Scald my gizzard, all the medicine I've ever needed is a bottle o' Shawnee Injun Oil and mebby a bag o' asafetida or a cup o' sage or tansy tea! 'Course, all an honest man ever has the matter with him is rheumatiz an' bunions. I'm tellin' you, if somebody don't get busy an' stop this Mowry quack, he'll be puttin' petticoats on every man an' makin' a nanny goat o' him, before he's finished. Believe me, if things get much worse 'n they now are, Rovin' Charley's goin' West — where a man's a man and freedom is still unmolested."

Mike lifted his chest and smiled. "Seems to me you're spreadin' your gravy pretty thick, Uncle Charley."

"Tarnation nonsense!" Roving Charley stamped his right foot vigorously. "Mike, if ever I find you lawin' or rottin' your stummick with vile medicine, I'll disown you."

Mike shrugged his shoulders and laughed. "Don't you lose any sleep, Uncle Charley." Suddenly Mike's face became serious, and he added: "There's just one thing I want to do, and only one thing! Whenever I close my eyes I keep seeing longhorns and flats, loaded with emigrant families, floating down the Ohio. Every night I dream I'm on a keelboat, fighting my way upstream, inching over every ripple. I'm just crazy to get my hands on a long oar, and my shoulder braced against an iron-shod pole. If I stay around here long, I'll soon be mustier than an old swamp moccasin. My mind is made up. It's the river for me."

Uncle Charley stretched his legs and crossed them comfortably. He twisted the ends of his mustache. "Well, lad, if your mind's really made up, I won't try to change it. But you can't blame an old trapper if he gives you a piece of his mind."

"Out with it," said Mike, sitting down on a homemade bench. "If you got anything on your chest, now's the time to unload it."

"If the bilin' sun don't get you, lad, the deceivin' sand bars, or the swirlin' suckin' eddies, or the bullyin' current will. Yes, and you're goin' to find every boatman flyin' the red feather in his cap, and carryin' a chip on his shoulder, waitin' for the excuse to claw an' bite an' gouge you to pieces. . . . You know somethin'? If I had my choice, I'd prefer bein' turned loose in a nest o' hungry wolves any day!"

"All I ask is half a chance, and the odds against me," said Mike, thumping his powerful fists against his resounding chest. "And then if I can't keep clear o' the sawyers and snags and sand bars, let me punch a hole in my boat an' go straight to the bottom."

"And remember this, young cock-a-doodle." Uncle Charley got up to ease his muscles. "Every minute you prolong a free-for-all fight-to-the-finish, the bigger chance you give the other feller to get the upper hand. Now here's a bottle o' b'ar grease I been savin' for you. Even a wild Injun knows that the best medicine in a fight is to keep your body slippery as a catfish so you can ease out o' tother feller's clutch."

Mike opened his shirt and laid bare his glossy shoulder. "This time I'm one jump ahead o' you. I've been greasin' my body regularly ever since I went scoutin' in the wilderness. . . . And while we're here together, Uncle Charley, I want to show you something else."

Mike led Uncle Charley out among the trees, and with his hunting knife cut a small round hole in the bark. He then stepped off ten paces, and drew a mark on the ground with his toe. He took the flat blade of his hunting knife between his thumb and forefinger, drew it back over his shoulder deliberately, and, with a quick overarm thrust and a deft flip of the wrist, threw his body forward. The knife flew swift as an Indian arrow, turned end-over-end once, and landed quivering, its point imbedded in the center of the mark.

Roving Charley clapped his hands and cackled in glee. "I never see a better pitch in my life."

"I learned this little game while I was scoutin' in the wilderness. I often killed small game this way. The Indians don't hear a hunting knife the way they do a gun."

Mike was grinning as he put his hunting knife back in its sheath. "And now with your permission, Uncle Charley, I'm goin' to show you something else." He set a nail in the side of the tree, and this time stepped off fifty paces. He sifted powder in his pan. He threw back his leg, and leveled his rifle at the mark. For a moment his tense body "froze" and the rifle remained rigid as if held in a vise. Then it spoke.

"Come along, Uncle Charley," Mike said, lowering his rifle. "Who knows, mebbe I missed the whole tree."

Roving Charley squinted his eyes, and when he saw that Mike had hit the nail square on the head and driven it home, he turned and slapped his nephew across the shoulder, exploding in falsetto laughter. "I'll be hornswoggled! You're sure a pizen shot with your Bang All! Why, Mike, you're one o' the Seven Wonders o' the World!"

"I'm no longer the child I once was, if that's what you mean."

Roving Charley's face grew serious. "All I can say, lad, is what you already know: Even though you travel down the river to the ends o' the world, my heart goes with you."

"Well, if you decide to move out o' this cabin, leave word with Ephraim Jones. I'll look you up soon as I get back from my first voyage."

"Mike, I'm mighty proud o' you." Uncle Charley's eyes narrowed to pin points. "An' if ever I hear o' you knucklin' under to any o' them cock-a-doodle-doo bullies, I'll never forgive you!"

"You've always been a father to me. . . . I'm grateful to you, Uncle Charley."

Tears welled up in Mike's eyes as they parted.

2. A Job on the *Half Moon*

Several hours later Mike walked with long firm strides to the Sign of the Catfish. His chin and chest were high, and his courage undaunted. Here he found five members of the crew of the *Half Moon* seated carelessly at the table, eating huge quantities of salt pork, hominy, and maple sugar. Each man was dressed in red shirt, blue-fringed surtout that reached almost to the knee, buckskin pantaloons, rough coonskin cap, moccasins, and red woolen sash. The men were in a jolly mood, and stopped eating long enough to sing to the squeaky melody of their gawky fiddler:

> Oh, the boatman is a lucky man,
> No one can do what the boatman can:
> The boatman can battle; oh, the boatman can sing;
> The boatman is up to everything;
> Yes, the boatman is up to everything. . . .

Blairsville Joint School Library
Blairsville, Pa.

The captain of the crew, Billy Earthquake, stood six feet five inches and held his chest high to exaggerate his stature. His coal-black hair fell in ringlets to his massive shoulders, and his skin, from long exposure to wind and rain and sun, shone as coppery as an Indian's. His nose was long and arched, and his mouth firm and strong. Withal, the captain was a kindly soul, and held his crewmen easily in the palm of his hand.

At Captain Billy's left sat his first mate, Micky Thunderbolt. Sawed off like an oak stump, Micky had the neck and chest of a gorilla, and his face carried the complete map of Old Ireland. At the slightest provocation, his feelings flashed up like powder in the pan. In fact, Micky loved a good fight more than he loved a good dinner, and so the crewmen allowed him the first chance to meet and subdue all comers.

Across the table sat Old Faithful Whirlwind, with a black patch over his left eye and his nose, souvenirs of a fight. His right eye radiated a greenish glare that was terrifying, and his hard face was set with deep rigid furrows like an eroded hillside.

Next after Old Faithful came High-Water-and-Certain-Death Creole Charley, a dusky giant whose muscles were like the knots of a curly maple. Two fingers were missing from his right hand, and he carried a deep hole in the middle of his forehead.

When the men had finished eating, Pappy the Mockingbird, whom they called "the Mocker," mounted the corner of the table. With bedraggled coonskin cap over his jaunty left ear and weather-beaten fiddle under his bewhiskered chin, he began sawing away at a ballad and teetering his toe to the beat of the melody. The Mocker was rawboned and horsy of face, and his front teeth showed like a muskrat's. Now that he was in a

mellow mood, he appeared harmless as a baby; but Mike wondered what wrath fell from him when he was angered.

As these men slouched and relaxed, they gave the appearance of adventurers bold as the besiegers of Ancient Troy. They were, in fact, the hardest, most powerful outfit of young boatmen to be found anywhere. With the exception of Old Faithful, the oldest was not above twenty-five years. Their carefree manners and unshaven weather-beaten faces made them seem as ageless as the river they sailed. Any lad with less courage than Mike's would have taken to his heels in fright at the sight of them.

While Mike looked each crewman up and down, Captain Billy called out to him with boisterous authority: "Step right over here, my young milksop, and have your fill from the fragments o' this feast."

"I'd rather not," said Mike, not stirring from his stool in the corner.

"A good meal'll help dry you off behind the ears," laughed Captain Billy.

"My purpose in coming here is to strike you for a job on your *Half Moon*," said Mike in a booming voice.

"A job it is he wants," cackled Micky, turning to see what kind of person Mike might be. "Listen, Cap'n Billy, listen to the bleat o' the young fawn for his mama!"

Captain Billy towered to his full height. "A job?" he chortled. "My advice to you, child, is simply this: Go back home to your mother for a few more moons till you've sprouted a man's beard. Then's the time we might talk about addin' you to the crew."

Micky drummed upon his chest with his fists. "You might

also tell the kid that the only way to land a job on the *Half Moon*'s to lick the stuffin' out o' our best fighter, which happens to be me, the one and only Micky Thunderbolt!"

Without waiting for a reply, Micky began waving his arms up and down and beating his open palms against his thighs, in imitation of a crowing rooster. "Cock-a-doodle-doo! I kin out-run, outhop, outskip, outjump any man in the world! I was reared on grizzly-b'ar milk, an' cradled with a wildcat. With one good grin, I kin blister a painter's heel. I kin return a b'ar's hug with compound interest, an' kin knock down a buffalo bull with one crack o' my good fist. I'm blood cousin to Hercules, an' full brother to the horse an' the alligator!"

Mike jumped to his feet and jerked off his buckskin shirt. "You're wasting a lot of good wind you'll be needing for this fight."

"I got 'nough wind left to crack the heads of a hundred beardless lads like you!" shouted Micky with menacing savagery.

Mike clenched his fists and hardened his jaw. "When you're ready, come on. If it's fisticuffs you're wantin', I'll give you your fill."

"I'll eat you alive," growled Micky, "easy as a catfish swallows a toad bait."

Without awaiting further insult, Mike threw himself like a flash of greased lightning at the fiery little Thunderbolt. Quicker than the keen eyes of the beholders could follow, Mike gave Micky a stinging left and right to the jaw. And while Micky was trying to count the flickering stars, Mike planted a smashing right — square on Micky's stubby nose. Before Micky regained his senses, Mike grabbed him by the heels and dragged him out through the tavern door. Everything was done with such assurance and precision that Captain Billy and his men stared openmouthed in astonishment. They half believed they were witnessing the visitation of the Devil himself, striking vengeance on their proud heads.

The next minute Mike bounced back into the tavern, drew a deliberate breath, and barked out at Captain Billy: "How many more of your men am I expected to knock down and drag out before you give me a place on your crew?"

Captain Billy came forward smiling. "By cracky, you're a brave lad!" He extended his hand to seal the bargain. "I'll give you the job you want." The captain's grip was like a vise, but Mike's closing palm apparently sent an answering shiver of pain to the captain's elbow.

Mike was now grinning from ear to ear. "With your permission, Captain Billy, I'll just run and fetch my long rifle and my hunting knife. You don't know it yet, but I'm what my Uncle Charley calls a 'pizen shot.' Mebbe I can provide a part of the meat we'll be needing on the voyage."

Captain Billy slapped him kindly across the shoulder. "You got a mighty good opinion of yourself, my lad. But run along, we never can tell when we may need extra firearms down the river."

Mike turned and fairly flew out of the door.

A short time later when Micky staggered back into the tavern, blowing his bloody nose and rubbing his stinging jaw, wondering if it had been broken, Captain Billy called out joyously: "Well, Micky, my lad, I've hired a new plug-ugly in the person of young Mike Fink."

Micky began to splutter, but Captain Billy raised his hand. "Keep quiet while I tell you of the scheme we've just been hatching while you been wallowing around in your own blood. We'll lay bets on young Mike same as we been laying on you, against the whole field of fighting cocks. And because Mike looks as stupid and harmless as a snapping turtle, we'll hold out for long odds, and win a mint of money."

Micky sulked. "Crack my lice, if only I'd knowed this was a wildcat 'stead of a flea-bitten rabbit, I coulda whipped him with one fist lashed behind me back."

"Hush your noise! You've not got the grain of sense you was born with!" roared Captain Billy. "So I'm telling you, you've at last met your master! The truth is, you're lucky to be alive after this explosion."

3. Rolling Down the Beautiful Ohio

Next morning at four o'clock Captain Billy ordered the bowlines cast off. The men in the galleys rowed the keelboat out into the current. Creole Charley and Old Faithful kept their places, each with his long oar "tossed," ready to help turn the boat whenever necessary. Captain Billy manned the heavy forty-foot sweep, and studied each movement of the surface water ahead.

The shadows of the trees and the hills were etched in the water along the shores. The birds sang. Only Mike and the Mocker saw and heard. The other men were busy with their morning chores. The Mocker sat atop the midship cargo box on a keg of salt pork, and leaned back against a barrel of corn meal. After he had tired of the scenery and the birds, he tucked his fiddle neatly under his bewhiskered chin, flexed his toe in time with the rhythm, and chanted an old ballad.

Hard upon the beach oar! . . .
She moves too slow!
All the way to Shawneetown,
Long while ago.
Sing *Hi ho-o-o*, jes' watch us go
Rollin' down the beau-ti-ful O-hi-o-o.

With no assigned task at the moment, Mike reclined at the Mocker's feet, relaxed by the lapping water and the warm sun and the rhythm of the music. Mike's eyes, however, from long months in the wilderness, were alert. He was watching for signs of wild game among the bushes and trees that skirted the shore. He admired Captain Billy's skill in managing the heavy sweep, and in locating every sawyer and wooden island and hidden snag that lay ahead. Two different times when Mike could see nothing that looked dangerous, Captain Billy shouted, "Man the oars, men. A steady pull."

Immediately, Creole Charley and Old Faithful set their oars firmly in the water and pulled long and steadily, while the Mocker set the rhythm with his fiddle.

"Mike, my lad," Captain Billy said kindly, "take a good look at the way the men in the galleys handle the oars. They set them down lightly with the current, and after a hard even pull they lift 'em without any drag. Hope you're not beginning to think this keelboating is a petticoat picnic, for it's not. Jes' wait till we turn back on the upstream voyage. Then you'll have to lay to with the rest o' the crew."

"Yes, sir, Captain Billy," said Mike with deep courtesy. "I'm keeping my eyes wide open. Any time you're in need of anything, you'll find me ready to do my part. In the meantime, if you're hankering for a turkey's wishbone or for a venison steak, maybe I can help you with Bang All."

"You don't mean to tell me," said Captain Billy, "that you can shoot a turkey or a deer from the deck o' this moving boat? I never heard tell o' such a crazy notion."

"I can't do less than make a try." Mike rammed a bullet home, sifted powder in his pan, and cradled Bang All across the crook of his arm.

The Mocker watched Mike's keen eyes follow back and forth along the shore. At that moment the keelboat happened to be floating past an outstanding landmark, a giant sycamore forty-seven feet in girth, its proud head so high it seemed a part of a forest above the forest.

"There's a cracking good story about this big tree that you ought to hear, Mike," said the Mocker, with a twinkle in his eye. "Some years ago, old Davy Crockett happened to be cruising along here at nightfall in his flat. Davy decided this spot was an excellent place to tie up for the night. So he cast his lines ashore and cuddled up in his buffalo robe expectin' to take a good night's sleep. About midnight Davy heard a terrific 'Snuff!' that set him up shiverin', for he knowed a giant b'ar was lookin' him over.

"As was his custom, Davy had a string o' catfish — some of 'em as big as fifty-pounders — danglin' over the side of his boat. Of course when Mr. B'ar scented the fish, he come straight after them. An' when Mr. B'ar set his forepaws on the gunwale o' Davy's flat, he come within half an inch o' capsizin' the craft. Mr. B'ar took the fish one at a time, and swallowed the biggest at a single gulp. This done, Mr. B'ar let out another 'Snuff!'

that sent the icy chills racin' up an' down Davy's tough spine.

"And when Mr. B'ar had finished off the last fish, he gave each o' Davy's shore lines one crack with his right forepaw, and parted 'em as if they was whipcord. Next thing Davy knowed, he heard the click o' claws, and understood Mr. B'ar was climbing that enormous sycamore tree.

"Naturally Davy's flat begun to drift, an' jes' as naturally it got itself snarled up in that eddy you see there at the foot of the giant tree. As soon as Davy'd begun to recover from his astonishment, he remembered his long rifle, Sweet Lips.

"Mebbe, Mike, you've heard tell o' Davy's powerful shooting iron, Sweet Lips. On the outside, it was somethin' the shape o' that plaything you got draped over your arm.

"Well, when his flat drifted around under the tree again, Davy naturally squinted at the b'ar, and grinned his durndest. Mebbe you've heard o' the way Davy could fetch the biggest varmint tumblin' out o' the highest branches with jes' one good long, steady grin. But this time, to Davy's surprise, nothin' happened. All Davy could see was two shining spots like Venus and Mars on a clear frosty night; only difference was these spots looked a hundred times brighter'n any stars ever could be.

"When his grin failed him, Davy poured half his flask o' powder down the muzzle o' his Sweet Lips, rammed home half a dozen bullets, pinted his gun up'ards between those two glowin' spots in the firmament, an' let 'er go.

"This time there was a 'Snuff!' that made all previous 'Snuffs!' seem like mere catfish grunts. Either the wind from this 'Snuff!' or the kick from overloaded Sweet Lips, or most likely both together, sent Davy flyin' overboard like a chip from the bite of a tomahawk.

[21]

"With his usual good luck, Davy succeeded in saving Sweet Lips — though this time he got both his gun an' his powder wet in the scuffle. But for once in his life old Davy Crockett knowed when he was licked, an' so he turned in an' went to sleep, plannin' to continue the fray next mornin'. Well, sir, at dawn, when he opened his peepers, Davy found, exactly as he had expected, that his flat was still adriftin' round an' round in that eddy; an' so Davy took a good look at that b'ar.

"At first Davy couldn't believe his eyes. What he saw was a b'ar jes' as much bigger'n the average b'ar as the giant sycamore was bigger'n the average trees of the forest. Davy carefully estimated this b'ar would easily measure five feet and a good twist o' Burley tobacker between the eyes, an' leastwise fifty-three feet from snout to tail.

"From long habit, but without serious thought o' the consequences, Davy let out another of his most fetchin' grins. Mr. B'ar turned his head deliberately, an' returned Davy's grin with compound interest, an' nearly bowled Davy headlong out o' his flat. An' as Mr. B'ar begun slidin' down the sycamore, he turned his head over his shoulder an' again grinned at Davy, an' let out the most terrific 'Snuff!' of all.

"Well, you can bet your last Spanish dollar 'gainst any man's thinnest twopence that Davy — famed b'ar hunter that he was — was scared, an' didn't lose any time steering his flat out o' that eddy. An' by the time Mr. B'ar reached the ground, Davy was a mile away, prayin' for a faster current. But even then, to Davy's practiced eye, Mr. B'ar looked like a movin' mountain.

"After this, for weeks on end, Davy couldn't get this enormous b'ar out o' his mind. He kept wonderin', over and over again a million times, how in the nation any b'ar could grow as big as this one. Finally, after great effort, Davy believed he had solved the riddle. Davy figured it out that Mr. B'ar and Mr. Sycamore must o' been playmates together during their childhood. An' when they were still youngsters, they must o' made a bet to see which could outgrow t'other. Each year thereafter, Mr. B'ar came back to prove to Mr. Sycamore that he could still shinny up his trunk, an' lift his head among the tallest branches.

"This, of course, meant that Mr. B'ar had to lengthen his legs as fast as Mr. Sycamore lengthened his girth, to be able to set his claws far enough around the expandin' trunk so that he didn't slip down faster'n he climbed up.

"As the centuries passed, the race went evenly on. An' so far as Davy could see, the race was likely to end, finally, in a tie."

While the Mocker spun this yarn, he cast many a sidelong glance to see what effect he was having on Mike. Mike was listening, but his eyes were as busy as frontier scouts. They were peering behind every shrub and tree, and as the keelboat drifted past a stretch of sandy beach, Mike gave a low resonant cluck. After two or three minutes he gave another cluck. Slowly he lifted Bang All to his shoulder, and steadily raised her muzzle. Deliberately he bent his trigger finger, and the sharp report echoed back and forth across the river. From behind a clump of willows, a great turkey gobbler leaped into the air and flopped its wings feebly.

As Mike swabbed out his gun, he smiled at Captain Billy: "There's your turkey wishbone, sir. Shall I take the canoe, and bring him aboard?"

"Well, I'll be flea-bitten to shreds if you're not a continual surprise party," said Captain Billy. "Micky, help the lad slip the canoe into the water."

Sometime later, Mike said quietly to the captain: "Would you like me to bring down a buck for you, sir?"

"Would I like a fresh venison steak?" said the captain with a smack of his lips. "By the time you're old enough to grow a crop o' whiskers, you'll never again ask such a foolish question. I never crave anything half as much as ven — "

The captain's last word was clipped short by the report of Bang All. While the echoes were still flying, the men looked in the direction Mike had pointed his rifle; saw a great antlered deer leap from behind a clump of elders, land in the splashing water, and start swimming madly toward the *Half Moon*. After a minute's struggle, the buck's proud antlers sank in the water.

"I must have plugged that old boy right through the heart," said Mike calmly. "Micky, will you please help me slip the canoe into the water again? I guess I better drag this fellow ashore. Save us a mess on deck."

While Mike was ashore cleaning the deer, Captain Billy said: "May the Devil cast me stone-blind if I didn't do a smart thing when I hired this beardless lad, even if I didn't need him on this sail downstream."

"Let the old gander take a lesson from the downy gosling, Mocker," laughed Micky. "Even a numbskull ought to know by this time Mike's not the child you can fool with a fairy tale about Davy Crockett."

Without paying the slightest attention to Micky's teasing, the Mocker sawed his squeaky fiddle and chanted with abandon:

Some rows up, but we float down,
All the way to Orleans town;

Pull away, my merry lads, pull away!
Sing *Hi ho-o-o*, jes' watch us go,
Floatin' down the beau-ti-ful O-hi-o-o.

When Mike returned with the venison, Captain Billy said, "Mike, I here and now appoint you Official Cookee o' the *Half Moon*. You'll serve under Micky and help him rustle the victuals."

Mike touched his cap in respectful salute. "Thank you, sir, this suits me fine."

Without waiting to be told, Mike kindled a fire on the clay platform in the center of the decked cargo box. And while Micky cooked the dinner, Mike jerked the venison, and began drying it before the fire.

"I see you're the one that don't have to be slapped in the face before you can see something to be done," said Micky with a chuckle. "I only hope that your fit o' workin' lasts."

After they had all taken their fill of food, Captain Billy asked Mike if he could read.

"I can manage to spell out a few words, sir."

"Very well, let me see what you can do with this Cramer's *Navigator*. . . . By the way, I don't suppose you've ever heard of the riverman's Testament?"

"Well, sir, I have — you see it's this way," said Mike. "Once I worked for Cramer, helping carry a wagonload of these books from his pressroom to his shipping department. He gave me a copy, and I've read it from cover to cover dozens of times. That was one reason I was so eager to join your crew and sail the river. I wanted to see with my own eyes all the interesting places Cramer described."

"Well, blister my heel, Mike," said Captain Billy in added

[25]

surprise, "if you're not the answer to a sailor's prayer! You see, I can't read, and not one of my crewmen can even spell his own name. You can't blame me for being curious to find out if Cramer knows as much as I do about where each of the hundreds of planters and sawyers and wooden islands lie."

Without further talk, Mike opened the *Navigator* and began to read:

Always navigate downstream in the center of the current. Exertion on the oars frequently throws the boat out of the current. The current itself carries the boat more rapidly, and is also the easiest course to steer. If you try to row faster than the current, you are likely to be thrown on the upper point of sand extending from an island before you are aware, or have time to regain the channel. Getting around this, you are likely to become entangled among aquatic timber, or tops or trunks of fallen trees. All this puts you in imminent danger. Only presence of mind and great exertion will extricate you. . . . In times of high water, it is best to land as seldom as possible — even keeping going at night. Trust the current and keep an alert lookout. . . .

Captain Billy nodded, "This is sound advice, right enough."

"Have you ever been thrown on the upper point of an island?" asked Mike.

"With your permission, Captain, I'll answer that one," laughed the Mocker, who with the other crewmen had been carefully listening to every word.

"When it comes to a yarn, Mocker, you win," Captain Billy grinned. "Your fool tongue's like a chattering water wheel — it keeps sputtering all the while, whether or not it has any grist to grind."

"You see it was like this, Mike," said the Mocker. "Some weeks ago Captain Billy was in such a hurry to get downstream that he could scarcely keep his shirt on. At the time we was carryin' a cargo of flour an' apple cider, with a smatterin' of plow irons, mill wheels, an' salt. The *Mornin' Star* would reach shippin' port ahead of us, an' spoil our market. So Captain Billy decided to race. He set all us men in the galley, an' commanded us to give him all we had. We rowed till we blistered our hands an' lamed our backs, but even then Captain Billy at the sweep was atearin' his hair out in fistfuls, an' shoutin' language so hot it singed all the elm trees for miles along the shore. The river was at spring freshet at the time, with water risin' so fast it was actually heaped up in the middle of the current.

"But in spite of all we could do, the *Mornin' Star* kept gaining on us every minute. There she came, ridin' the current as unconcerned as a wild swan. Here we was abustin' our sides pullin' at the long oars, the wind whistlin' in our oars, and there the *Mornin' Star* was adriftin' by us while her crewmen sat about on deck, laughin' at us fit to kill.

" 'Where d' you think you're goin' in such a terrible hurry?' shouted Captain Butler of the *Mornin' Star*. 'Cast us your cordelle, an' we'll be glad to tow you anywhere you say.'

"This tauntin' made Captain Billy so all-fired hot that his breath next to burned us all to a cinder.

"Well, in the middle of our excitement, first thing we knowed, we struck a sand bar at the head o' Sugar Island, an' come to a stop with a terrific jolt that sent our cargo bouncing all over the place. An' to make bad matters worse, our prow was high an' dry, and our stern deck only an inch from bein' under water. An' there we hung betwixt heaven an' hell, havin' to watch the proud *Mornin' Star* wave her tail feathers at us as she rolled on ahead, an' vanished around the next curve in the channel.

"And believe me, before we cleared that sand bar, there wasn't any apple cider left to sell. We'd gulped it down a gallon at a swallow, while we were puddlin' round in the surging water up to our chins, pryin' an' pushin' an' haulin' every which way, till we'd strained every timber in our boat.

"And blast our luck, we was no sooner off the sand bar than we drifted onto what Cramer calls 'aquatic timber.' Well, to make a long story short, by the time we had regained the current, we was all so exhausted that we slumped down in our bunks an' told Captain Billy he could navigate this fool boat down the river by himself or wreck her on the next hidden sawyer, jes' as he jolly well pleased. For all we cared, we was through till we'd caught up on our sleep. Captain Billy scorched us aplenty with his hot blasts, but we snuggled down from sheer weariness, and went to sleep.

"And what do you think, you beardless child? Strike me blind, if we didn't teach our fool captain a good lesson in navigation. While we was all asnoring under his very nose, he found out the fastest way to sail a boat downstream was to let the craft float with the current. Now, wasn't that somethin'?"

"The old Mocker is tellin' the truth this time," chuckled Captain Billy. "That was about the biggest single lesson I ever learned in navigation. Keep ahold of your sweep, lad, and nose your boat down the center of the current, same as I'm doing this very minute. Nature does better for you than anything you can do for yourself. An' take it from Captain Billy, this is the Gospel truth."

As Mike continued to read from the *Navigator*, Captain Billy frequently interrupted him.

"I didn't realize, until you read Cramer," said Captain Billy, "how fast the river keeps changing her fool mind. No wonder many sailors call her a flirting, rattlebrained girl! After every freshet, she shifts her planters and sawyers and wooden islands. Often she suddenly decides to plant new ones at the most unexpected places. And at times she even changes her current.

"Now here's a sawyer right in front o' your nose," continued Captain Billy. "You can see him here now on our larboard, wagging his fool head up and down in derision, leering wickedly at us. Micky first discovered him last year, and named him St. Peter. This particular smarty happens to be the same elm we used as a marker on the shore there behind us, where you can see that fresh cave-in. This sawyer was thrown into the river by the flood tide a year ago this May. You can see for yourself, Mike, it's one that's not mentioned by Cramer. Of course this Cramer's a mighty help to a young navigator, even though the book is always a year or two behind the times. The only sure guide, Mike, is your own brainpan. A man has to keep a steady look-around every time he has a date with the flirting old gal, and even then she often deceives him."

While they talked, the *Half Moon* floated down the current between the rocky rugged hills at the left and the deep virgin woodlands on the right. At frequent intervals the *Half Moon* passed long-horns and flats with emigrant families aboard. And often the river flowed in silence between endless stretches of unexplored wilderness.

4. Whipping the Rattlesnake and Winning the Raffle

One afternoon at Wheeling, Captain Billy ordered the bowlines ashore, and tied up alongside numerous other river craft.

Mike mingled with the milling crowd of boatmen, trappers, and scouts. The boat captains bartered their wares with the merchants, but the crowd in the street was as hilarious as boys just out from school. Many of the boatmen were drinking heavily, while others were exchanging experiences and sharing wild tales of the wilderness.

When the shades of night fell, the fun really did begin. At one end of the wharf an excited group placed bets on a cockfight. Just beyond, another group was gambling with cards. In front of the village tavern, mounted on a bench behind a flour barrel, stood a thimble-rig magician. He was barking at the crowd, and wagering that no man could guess under which of three thimbles he had placed a pea. His agile fingers kept the pea moving and the crowd excited.

Mike watched silently while five different men lost money, and decided it was never safe to bet on the other fellow's game. Farther down the street two men were tangling in a rough-and-tumble fight, while the crowd screeched and yelled. This was a fight with no rules save the dictates of savagery, and the loser was likely to be disfigured for life.

Mike was all eyes and ears. The frontier melee was making an indelible impression. He had entirely forgotten Micky, who at the moment was laying bets with all takers that young Mike could whip the Rattlesnake of the Ohio, reputed to be the fiercest bully anywhere around.

Presently Mike found himself facing a scowling, sputtering, shirtless giant. With arms flapping at his sides, the bully was crowing his brag: "I'm the one and only pizen Rattlesnake of the O-hi-o-o. . . . I can outfight any man this side o' Kingdom Come!"

"Shut your trap, you big bully!" growled a man from the crowd.

Another shouted, "Why don't you pick on somebody your size?"

"You're nothing but a cradle robber and murderer!" shrieked a third.

Mike saw all eyes were focused on him, and knew the only honorable way out was to play the game. He jerked off his shirt, and imitated the neigh of a charging stallion. This, in the language of the frontier, meant that he accepted the challenge.

"Hold off your thunderous attack," shouted still another hoarse voice.

"I'm not bullyin' the kid," hissed the Rattlesnake. "It's a fair fight, an' no holds barred. So shut up your jawin'!"

"Make the circle bigger," shouted Micky, rushing around and waving his arms, and pushing back the crowd. "Give the lad a fair chance to show his stuff!"

Without warning, the Rattlesnake crouched, with arms alert, and made a mad rush for Mike. Quicker than greased lightning Mike sidestepped. The Rattlesnake hesitated an instant in confusion, and in that split second Mike landed a sledge-hammer right to the base of his ear. This was a blow to bring a giant to his knees, and the Rattlesnake tottered under the impact.

Mike followed up his advantage with a pair of uppercuts to the giant's chin, and three sledge-hammer blows to his nose. The Rattlesnake went down like a felled oak.

The mob was struck silent as if by an electric shock. Each man stood gaping.

A minute later when the Rattlesnake slowly lifted himself to his knees and bellowed he'd now get even with the kid, Mike neatly landed another hammer blow to the base of the ear. This laid the Rattlesnake cold for half an hour, and ended the battle.

Thus Mike became a sensation among the rivermen. He was a new kind of fighting man. His fighting was clean and sharp as a razor blade, and surer than the strike of a snapping turtle, and deadlier than a mule's heel.

When the men had recovered from their first astonishment, they cheered Mike until they were too hoarse to speak. While they cheered, Micky laid an affectionate arm across his shoulder, and bellowed in his ear, "I knowed the Rattler couldn't last

a minute with you. This ought to learn that old billy goat to look twice before he butts into another stranger."

This fight was just the beginning of Mike's fame. Whenever he met a crowing rooster, Micky would lay as many bets as possible, and Mike would be forced to fight. He was so quiet in appearance and so explosive in action that the rivermen named him "the Snapping Turtle of the O-hi-o-o." Without Mike's knowing it, his name and fame began to flash across the frontier heavens like a meteor. Wherever rivermen congregated, someone was sure to tell some tall story about the beardless boy wonder: how he held a thunderbolt in each separate fist, and conquered the fiercest cock-a-doodle with a single crashing blow.

A few days later the *Half Moon* docked at Louisville. As usual at every pier, a knot of buckskin-clad men were swapping yarns of hunting, trapping, and shooting. Tacked up on the warehouse was this announcement:

> Thomas Crabtree will conduct a raffle for a prime beef at the Crabtree clearing a mile up the Branson Flour Mill trail. A separate match will be held for each quarter, and one for the hide. Each marksman will be allowed one shot in each match he wishes to enter. The price for each chance is one shilling. Shooting begins at one o'clock Saturday afternoon, May the sixth. Come one, come all. The more the merrier. Your chance to win is just as good as the next fellow's. . . .

"While Captain Billy's fillin' out his cargo," said Micky to Mike, "we'll get permission to attend the raffle. We'll buy you a ticket on each of the five matches, and this'll give you the chance to win all the prizes."

As they drew near the scene of the raffle Micky loitered behind. He didn't wish anyone to know that he was Mike's friend when he started laying bets.

The clearing around the Crabtree cabin was crowded with frontiersmen. They had come from far and near, some as far as a three-day journey.

Mike found Crabtree, tall and straight as a wagon tongue, standing beside a great cottonwood stump, selling chances. He was clad in heavy woolen coat, buckskin leggings and ribbed woolen stockings, the handiwork of his wife. His beaded Indian moccasins were high, and his soft wool hat was cocked up on one side and held a buck-tail plume.

Beside him, leaning carelessly on his long weather-beaten rifle, stood Simeon Maitland, a renowned scout. His butternut coat had been cut from a Government blanket. His breeches and moccasins were fashioned from buckskin. His pouch and powderhorn, slung across his chest, showed long wear, as did his coonskin cap, the ringed tail dangling behind to his shoulders. His clear gray eyes were kindly.

Mike lost no time in buying his chances. When he handed Crabtree his money, the manager of the raffle looked Mike over from head to foot and said:

"You're a youngish lad to be wastin' all your hard cash on chances."

"Excuse me, Mr. Crabtree," said Mike, smiling, "but I believe it's my own money."

"You're right, there, sonny," drawled Crabtree. "My conscience is now clear, for I've give' you good an' fair warnin'. Mebbe you don't know it, my lad, but we got right here in this clearing a hundred o' the pizenest shots in the whole state o'

Kentuck, an' that's same as sayin' the deadliest shots in the whole world."

Mike took up his chance for each separate match. "Even these old master hands don't scare me, Pappy."

After Mike had scrawled his name on the list of marksmen, Crabtree spelled it out: "M-i-k-e F-i-n-k — Mike Fink; am I right?"

"You are."

"An unknown name to these parts. Sounds Scotchlike and it also sounds Irish. I never yet have known any stranger bearin' this particular moniker."

"Only give me time," said Mike calmly. "I aim to make the name well known within a few years."

"A young cock-a-doodle acrowin' before you've growed a decent stand of whiskers," cackled Crabtree. "Glad to meet a man-child with so much confidence. Where you hail from?"

"From Fort Pitt," said Mike, with an affectionate glance at Bang All.

"A longish way from home for such a striplin' lad."

"Don't be too hard on the lad," said Maitland, running his hand lovingly along the barrel of his long rifle. "When I was Mike's age I could shoot the eye out of a turkey gobbler at a hundred yards, ninety-nine times out of a hundred."

"I don't pretend to be that good," said Mike with a shrug, "but I thank you for your kind words."

"That was years ago. I'm not that good now, either. My hands are not as stiddy as they once were."

The match was about ready to start. The chairman of the committee of judges was Pete Wherry, affectionately known as "the Father of Raffle Shootin' in Kentuck." He wore the uniform coat of the Chartiers Riflemen, the company of Home Guards of which he was the captain. The other judges were John Barnes, keeper of the Sign of the Wild Pigeon, and Dick Kirk, a gunsmith from Louisville.

The targets were made from slabs, fresh-split from clear white oak. In the center of each was set a hand-wrought nail. These were set up in a row at the edge of the clearing.

"Draw near for the first match!" called Wherry in a clear voice.

The thirty-nine men who had bought chances took turns firing at the target at fifty yards. Mike hit his nail square on the head and easily qualified as one of the eight best marksmen to try for the final round.

The first contestant called was the old scout, Simeon Maitland. As he came forward with long easy strides, he called out to a friend, but loud enough for all to hear, "When I shot again' Dan'l Boone down at Mayville thirteen year ago this comin' July the first, I want you to know I run Dan'l a close second. Yes, sir-ee, I even beat him by an eyelash in one match."

"Thirteen year is plenty long enough to fill yer rear sight with rust," bantered Thomas Porter. "I'll bet you two shillin' you don't hit the nail square on the head today."

"I'll bet you I'll at least bend the nail," said Simeon.

"Bendin' yer nail's not good enough to win beef in this raffle," added Henry MacDougle.

"I'll bet you your two shillin', Henry," said Simeon as he squinted through his sights, "that I come closer to the nailhead than you do."

"An' I'll jes' bet the winner four shillin'," countered Tom, "that I come closer'n either o' you."

"Quit yer banterin' an' get down to business," growled Harry Cartwright, growing impatient. "Get your bushy whiskers off the trail, so the rest o' us can take our turn. You may jes' as well shet your eyes an' blaze away in the dark, for you've got no chance o' winnin' anything nohow."

This talk brought exclamations of both delight and impatience from the two lanes of spectators, craning their necks to get a clear view.

Without noticing his hecklers, Simeon examined his flint, and wiped out the pan of his Merry Weather. He lifted his gun slowly and squinted along its sights a second time. Then he lowered Merry Weather, flicked a grain of dust from the barrel, blew a hard breath through the rear sight. He sifted powder in the pan. Taking a different stance, he raised the barrel deliberately, and squeezed the trigger.

The judges examined the charred target, and Pete Wherry announced, "Simeon's nicked the head and bent the nail, but he's an eighth-inch from the dead center o' his nailhead."

Simeon examined his target carefully, shook his head sadly: "When I was shootin' against Dan'l Boone, I averaged a lot better than this, every time I shot. I must be a little out o' practice, but I'll be doin' better my next shot."

The second man called was Thomas Porter, a florid moon-faced homesteader. Thomas toyed lovingly with his firing piece, raised it nervously to his shoulder and took it down. He spread his feet rather too far apart, drew a deep breath, raised his barrel quickly, and fired.

This time Pete Wherry announced: "Tom's an eighth-inch

further from dead center than Simeon. He's jes' managed to nick his nail. Better luck to you next time, Tom."

It was now Henry MacDougle's turn. Henry was short and stocky, and more deliberate than a sluggish porcupine. After toying for five minutes with his Lucky Provider, Henry finally took his stance, and fired.

Pete Wherry announced loud and clear, "Hen, you're a sixteenth of an inch from the nailhead."

The shooting went on and on. No marksman had missed his nail farther than an inch. As Mike's turn drew near, Micky slyly began to lay bets.

"No difference how close anybody else comes to the bull's-eye," said Micky, "I'm bettin' one to two young Mike'll win this match. Against the whole field, one to two is big odds."

"You don't mean you're bettin' on that young gamecock yonder?" asked Henry MacDougle.

"Yes sir-ee," Micky whispered. "You jus' won four shillin', an' I'm bettin' you two and sixpence against your four that Mike wins this match."

"I'll take you up on that." Henry smacked his lips. "I may as well pick up an extra shillin' now and then as not."

Micky went quietly from one contestant to the other, and then to the onlookers, and when he could not get odds, he bet even money on Mike.

Finally, when his name was called, Mike stepped up as relaxed as if he had nothing at stake. Quickly he poured powder from his horn into his charger and thence into Bang All's long barrel. He next patched his bullet and drove it home with one long even thrust of his hickory ramrod. He sifted powder into his pan.

The older men smiled with approval at the carefree expertness of Mike's movements. Without even pausing, Mike drew back his foot and raised Bang All to his shoulder. When he saw the nailhead through his sights, his body "froze," and for a split second the rifle was stationary, as if held in a vise. Automatically he crooked his finger, and the sharp report echoed back and forth across the clearing.

Pete Wherry exclaimed: "Well, of all the miracles I've ever witnessed! This beardless lad has hit his nail square on the head and driven it home."

When the match was over, the judges announced that Mike had easily won.

There was wagging of heads and an astonished silence. After a few minutes Simeon Maitland sniffed, "Beginner's luck, that's jes' what it is. It can't happen again."

"True enough," added Tom Porter: "lightnin' seldom strikes twice in the same place."

"Never in all my long experience," agreed Simeon, "have I seen it strike twice in the same place, not since I see Dan'l Boone shoot sixteen year ago."

"Slap me down for bein' a fool," groaned Henry MacDougle, "here I let myself go an' lose four good shillin' o' hard money on a baby."

"Shet up, you tightwad of a Scot," laughed Simeon. "It was my money you handed over to Micky. You haven't lost a twopence."

"If any o' you want to lose a few more shillin'," whispered Micky behind Mike's back, "I'll bet you even money that this boy wonder wins the second match jes' as easy as he won the first."

When the second match was finally over, the judges again announced that Mike Fink was the only contestant to hit the nail square on the head.

Again there was wagging of heads and deep astonishment. This time Micky had no trouble laying bets for the next match, for everyone was positive Mike couldn't win three times in a row. It just wasn't within the law of human probability.

The third match, however, proved that the impossible could happen. Mike again hit the nail square on the head.

By this time, judged by frontier values, Micky was next thing to a millionaire. Each loser now demanded that Micky bet two to one on the fourth match. It just wasn't possible that any contestant could win four matches in succession. Micky pretended he wanted to quit betting, but allowed himself to be coaxed into laying one bet after another.

When young Mike Fink won the fourth match, the astonishment of the crowd turned to wonder — and even to fear.

"Must be the youth is under the spell o' some evil spirit an' has us all bewitched," grumbled Simeon Maitland. "He's shootin' like a god that can't miss the mark. I been shootin' in matches all my life, an' I never see anybody 'ceptin' Dan'l Boone win so many in a row — an' even Dan'l's record was but three."

"There's some hidden hitch somewheres," added Tom Porter, beginning to get mad. "They's something crooked goin' on 'round here that we're not smart 'nough to see."

"I'm a broke man," moaned the canny MacDougle.

Mike happened to overhear this last statement, and said with a quiet grin, "You still got your shirt, haven't you, Mr. MacDougle? Well, I'm givin' you the chance to win something easy. I'll bet you this last hindquarter I've just won against your shirt that I win this last match for the hide."

Henry hesitated, and while he was trying to find some excuse, Simeon bantered, "You old tightwad of a pack horse, I hope you're not goin' to let this upstart of a young colt chase you out o' the pasture lot."

Rather than stand the jeers of the crowd, Henry MacDougle placed the bet. While this byplay was going on, Micky was placing every wager he could make on the final match.

Simeon Maitland, taking his stance in the fifth and final match, said to Tom: "What am I skeered about? Didn't I once beat Dan'l Boone?" In a supreme effort, Simeon hit his nail squarely on the head. "Even Mike Fink can't beat this shot," laughed Simeon when Pete Wherry made the announcement. All his friends congratulated Simeon on his victory.

When Mike's turn came, he lifted his Bang All, and with seeming unconcern, drove the nail home with a perfect bull's-eye.

The judges finally quieted the turmoil and announced that the tie would have to be shot off. In a clear voice, Pete Wherry called, "Mike Fink will shoot first this time."

Mike took time out to wipe the burned powder from his barrel before ramming his bullet home. Just as Mike drew his foot back and was lifting Bang All to his shoulder, Henry MacDougle, thinking to unnerve the lad, shouted, "Simeon Maitland wins this match or I'm no Scotchman."

While Mike lowered his gun and took another stance, Tom remarked dryly, "I'm sorry for you, MacDougle, for I'm sure the Irish and the English will never claim you for one of their own."

Mike now brought Bang All steadily into position, and squeezed the trigger. The judges examined the target with the greatest of care before announcing, "Of all the Seven Wonders of the World . . . Mike Fink's again hit the nail square on the head!"

This shot so unnerved Simeon that he twiddled and faltered, brought his Merry Weather to his shoulder and lowered her down a dozen different times. He flicked imaginary dust from her barrel. Finally, he held his aim so long that he was nervous as a witch when at last he squeezed the trigger.

After the judges had examined the target, Pete Wherry announced, "Sorry, Simeon, but you've lost by a sixteenth-inch."

An ominous murmur ran through the crowd, and for a minute or two it seemed a riot would break out.

Thomas Crabtree sensed this. He came forward quickly and grasped Mike's hand. "Young Mike Fink, you've shot fair and you've won clean," he said in a voice for all to hear. "You're sure the best shot ever seen in these parts."

"I told you I aimed to make my name known round these clearings," said Mike quietly, "only I'm surprised it has happened so soon."

To avoid trouble, Micky quickly gathered his final winnings, sauntered nonchalantly until he was out of sight behind the cabin, then ran for his life through the woods to the *Half Moon*. Safely within the cabin, he emptied his bulging pockets. "What you know!" he said to himself. "I got here enough money to set both Mike and me up in business. I'll sew half of it in the linin' of my clothes, an' relax on my pallet till Mike gets here."

Back at the scene of the matches, young Mike quieted the hostile crowd. "Mr. MacDougle," he called out in his booming voice: "we'll just forget about our little wager. What you say?"

Henry shook Mike's hand. "Mighty white o' you, Mike."

"And you, Simeon Maitland," Mike added: "Bang All was sure poison today. I couldn't miss anything. You tied me in that last match — and I hope you'll let me make you a present o' this hide."

Simeon swallowed hard. "You're doin' all right, Mike, even if you've not got too many whiskers." He cleared his throat. "I got a sister in a lonely cabin. She lost her man last year. She an' her chilluns all need moccasins, an' this hide'll come in mighty handy."

"I got no use for it," said Mike, "so take it right along."

Simeon shook hands with Mike. "Thanks," he said.

"Listen, you other men who've shot against me!" said Mike, raising his voice. "This hindquarter's all the beef I can use. You men are at liberty to draw lots to see who's lucky enough to carry home the other pieces of meat. Pete Wherry, you an' the other judges will please carry on from here."

Mike shouldered his hindquarter of beef, and as he left the clearing he couldn't help hearing what the men were saying.

"I'll be hog-tied an' hornswoggled!" said one.

Another said, "It jes' don't seem possible it coulda happened."

"You're right," said a third. " It'll be jes' my luck to wake up in the mornin' an' find this is all a fool dream."

5. The Young Alligator-Horse

Below Louisville lay two miles of the river's most treacherous rapids, the falls of the Ohio. There white waters laughed and leaped and swirled between jagged, hidden rocks on either side of the navigable chute. Any craft that strayed from the narrow, tortuous channel was quickly torn to pieces.

Mike was tense as a bowstring as he sat opposite the Mocker in the galley, his long oar "tossed," awaiting Captain Billy's command. Micky, his long spiked pole in hand, stood in the stem of the boat, ready for any emergency. Captain Billy, his feet braced, the long heavy sweep in his two hands, navigated the *Half Moon* cautiously into the swift stream leading into the Indian Chute, near the Indiana shore.

Mike expected the worst as the *Half Moon* was sucked into the leaping current, and sped forward with the reckless ease of a plunging salmon. Captain Billy, sensing every hidden rock and every turn in the corkscrewing channel, pulled and pushed the heavy sweep fast as flashes of lightning. The oarsmen in the galley eyed him like hawks, swaying and tossing with the boat, drawing a sharp deep breath at every scrape of the keel on bedrock.

The ten minutes seemed a year to young Mike. When the *Half Moon* leaped from the last riffle, and settled down in the smooth-flowing current, he rested his oar as did the others, and flicked the sweat from his forehead.

"Whew!" he said to Mocker. "That was sure some race!"

"Three cheers for Cap'n Billy," shouted Micky. "Hurrah! Hurrah! Hurrah!"

"You didn't miss keepin' *Half Moon* down dead center o' the chute, not even by the width o' one o' Mike's thin whiskers," said the Mocker.

Old Faithful chimed in, "You're sure ace-high amongst river pilots."

"Right you all are," said Creole Charley, smiling in childlike delight.

Captain Billy was pleased. Bestriding the heavy sweep, he relaxed his arms and grinned. "There's nothin' to it, mannees. The trick is, I always carry a rabbit's-foot in my pocket."

Relieved from the strain, the men put aside their oars, and each went about his accustomed duties. Amidship, on the cargo box, the Mocker took up his fiddle and chanted:

> Sing *Hi ho-o-o*, jes' watch us go
> Rollin' down the beau-ti-ful O-hi-o-o.

A spanking breeze struck astern, and Captain Billy shouted, "Hoist sail!"

The boat ran down the current at a merry pace.

Captain Billy was in a pleasant mood. He had taken such a liking to young Mike that he decided to teach him the fine art of piloting the boat. Gesturing with his forefinger, he said, "Laddie, come over here. I got somethin' I want to show you."

"Yes, sir," said Mike, touching his cap.

"Take my place for a while here at the sweep. The current runs straight as a ramrod for quite a ways. First thing you got to learn is the feel o' the sweep in your hands an' the feel o' the boat under you. Steady now, you're pushin' her over a wee bit too hard. That's better. You're a keen lad, an' you'll get the sleight o' navigatin' in no time."

Whenever they approached a difficult riffle or a dangerous sucking current, Captain Billy said, "Step aside a minute, Mike, watch how the trick is turned. There's nothin' much to handlin' the sweep, once you hit on the knack."

"You sure do make easy work of it," said Mike, again trying his hand.

"Look now, do you see that swirl in the water ahead? What does it say to you?"

"It might tell me there's a large boulder down under."

"Could be just that, but I happen to know it's the wreck o' the *Redstone*. Last year she hit a hidden snag, an' sunk so fast the crew saved nothin' but their yawl."

A half hour later they approached Murphy's Left Knee.

"Young Mike," said Captain Billy, "see anything ahead?"

"Looks like a big whirlpool."

"That's right, an' what does it say to you?"

"It must say there's a hole in the bottom o' the river."

Captain Billy slapped his thigh and laughed. "Must be the Mocker's been tellin' you his yarn about holes that go down all the way to China! But don't believe a word he says. This is the start of a strong undercurrent that comes foaming to the surface around the bend. Beware of all whirlpools and steer clear o' them. If we should allow ourselves to be sucked into this one, we'd find we were caught in a nasty rapids and flung like a helpless chip on the rocks below. We'd be tossed high an' dry, and our voyage would come to a sudden end."

This was but the first lesson. Whenever Mike had nothing else to do, Captain Billy would take him in hand, and impart his wisdom.

Gradually the channel of the Ohio widened. The steep hills along its banks disappeared. Heavy forests crowded its shores, and dark overhanging trees closed them in from the outside world. Green-clad, low-lying islands often divided the current. Planters and sawyers were likely to be strewn anywhere. Young Mike marveled at Captain Billy's uncanny sensing of every change in the channel and of every fresh or shifted obstruction.

Finally the *Half Moon* reached the mouth of the Ohio, and Mike thrilled at the sight of the mighty Mississippi extending for what seemed miles in every direction. Eddies large and small swirled on all sides. Currents and countercurrents struggled for mastery.

"How are you ever going to find your way through all this angry water?" asked Mike.

"That's easy, laddie. Just watch how I do it, an' you'll see. Fortunately the wind's right. The sail'll carry us where we want to go."

Mike's eyes were wide. He tried to see everything at once. He couldn't understand how Captain Billy could be so cool and so sure of the direction. But sure enough, through the snarling maze of currents the *Half Moon* was finally brought into the sweep of the Father of Waters.

"Now, Mike, we're astride a river what is a river," said the Mocker, laying his fiddle across his knees. "If you think the Ohio a beautiful but fickle girl, you'll find the Massassip a lurin' siren and a greedy harpy, all in one package. One minute she'll charm you with her quiet homelike ways. When she's got you dreamin' in bliss, she'll lure you into her treacherous shallows or wreck you on her swirlin' riffles. One day she'll bathe you in golden sunshine. Next thing you know, she's lashin' you with blindin' torrents o' rain an' hail. Then she'll drive you crazy with swarms o' mosquitoes big as hummingbirds, with beaks that can drill the hide of an alligator or the hoof of a buffalo. When she has you about ready to die, she'll make you happy by droppin' apples o' gold in your boat. One day she brings you peace an' plenty, an' the very next she racks you with fever an' ague somethin' terrible. She's always tryin' to break a man's heart by the time she's finished with him." He stopped a minute, and a smile filled his twinkling eyes. "But, Mike, if you truly love sailin', you'll never be happy with any other life, even though the siren keeps you lashed to the mast most of the time."

"That's no way o' talkin' about the flirtin' old girl," said Micky. "You know you can't help admirin' her, even though she's always tryin' to trick you."

Mike didn't say anything, but he thought a lot. He was in love with the river, the "fickle ol' girl." That was all he knew and all he cared to know.

[50]

A month later Captain Billy tied up at Natchez-under-the-Hill. He sent Micky and Mike ashore to round up a few extra crewmen for the return voyage, while he bartered his wares and laid in a profitable cargo of coffee and Orleans molasses.

The street was an inferno of wild rivermen. "Looks like a dozen young Wheelings," said Mike, "all scufflin' and fisti-cuffin' each other."

Micky grinned. 'She's worse'n that even."

They watched at least twenty different fights through to the end, and talked to the hardiest fighters. When Micky wasn't certain about the quality of a prospective crewman, he picked a personal quarrel. And when he wasn't sure he could whip the man himself, he laid a bet that young Mike, the frontier boy wonder, could do the job.

Mike brought half a dozen hard customers into quick sub-mission, and attracted a lot of attention.

"Here's a snag you would do better to avoid," shouted a bystander. "He's a snag that rips the ribs off your keel 'fore you know what's happenin'."

"You're right," shouted another. "This young cock-a-doo-dle's the most dangerous snag on the ol' Massassip!"

Others quickly took up the name, and when the men scattered, they spread wild tales of "the Snag of the Massassip."

When the *Half Moon* headed upstream, Captain Billy said with dry humor: "The downstream voyage was a Sunday picnic the whole of the way. The time has come, mannees, to show me you got enough gravel in your gizzards to make good use of the oars an' poles, an' the cordelle." (He meant the towrope.)

"We'll stick to you, Captain Billy, through thick an' thin,

to the end of the voyage," said Micky, "faithful as Natchez clay to our moccasins."

During the first miles of the voyage, the river lay wide as the ocean and calm and placid as a millpond. Captain Billy set his men at the oars, and navigated *Half Moon* just outside the main current, where at times he had the aid of an upstream eddy. But he still kept young Mike at his side, whenever possible, and gave him a chance at the tiller.

The keelboat moved steadily forward across Petit Gulf and then skirted Bayou Pierre. Only trouble was that the crewmen were nearly eaten alive by swarms of big black mosquitoes.

"Your face an' hands an' neck look like the smallpox, Mike," said the Mocker. "This'll learn you to grow more whiskers. Why, I once knowed a young sprout so skeered o' mosquitoes that he growed a yard o' whiskers durin' a single upstream voyage. Soon his beard got so long he had to braid it an' tie the strands behind his back to keep from stumblin' over them when he walked."

Micky grinned. "Don't you worry none 'bout Mike. If you use your eyes you can see whiskers coarse as a wolf's mane breakin' out all over his face."

Later, when the river narrowed and the current proved too strong for the oars, the crewmen were forced to bushwhack. Captain Billy navigated the boat close to shore and the men tugged at the branches of the overhanging willows and cypress. This gave Mike the chance to put his powerful muscles to good use. Slowly but surely the keelboat was pulled past Nine Mile Reach.

Hull's Left Leg gave Captain Billy the chance to make use

of a mile-long upstream eddy. The men rowed and the keelboat moved forward with speed. Spanish Moss Bend they also passed easily. Paddy's Hen and Chickens (one large and a dozen smaller islands in a row) divided the current and made the going perilous.

When they reached the Devil's Raceground, Captain Billy set his men ashore, gave them all they could eat, and let them rest for three hours. For the first half mile after that they took advantage of another upstream eddy. When this ended, Captain Billy swung the *Half Moon* abruptly toward the opposite shore.

"Man your oars, an' give 'em all you got!" shouted Captain Billy. "An' may the devil take any laggard!"

The men gave their last ounce of strength — Mike outdoing all the others — and Captain Billy threw his powerful muscles against the heavy sweep. Together they held the *Half Moon* from being sucked into the raging current. But in spite of all they could do, they drifted three quarters of a mile downstream.

For the next two miles the men were again forced to bushwhack, and at the end of four hours they reached the rapids.

"Stand to your poles!" shouted Captain Billy.

Half of the men lined up on one side of the deck, and half on the other side, each with his pole tossed, ready for instant action.

"Set poles!"

Each man dropped the iron-tipped end of his pole over the side of the boat and set it firmly on the river bed.

"Down on poles!"

Each man placed the button end of his pole against the leather pad at his shoulder, bent low, and forced his way from stem to stern with the greatest effort. As the foremost man on each side reached the stern, Captain Billy shouted, "Lift poles!" The two men obeyed, and hurried back to the stem over the runners. Again they set their poles firmly, and slowly worked their way back to the stern. Thus the crewmen were in constant motion, somewhat like a human caterpillar tractor tread.

Beneath them the keelboat crept forward. Sweat ran down their faces, and the muscles of their legs and backs knotted under the intense strain. Above the heavy breathing, Old Faithful wheezed like an overdriven wind-broken horse. Mike alone had the strength and stamina to enjoy the ordeal.

One slight mishap unbalanced the smooth teamwork. As Creole Charley crouched low above the cleated deck and gave his last ounce of strength, his iron-tipped pole slipped between the water-washed rocks on the river bed. When his pole again struck firm footing, he was thrown so heavily forward that his pole snapped in the middle, hurtling him headlong into the water.

Captain Billy was prepared for just such an emergency. He shouted, "Hold 'er steady, mannees!" He grabbed up another pole, threw it wide on Creole Charley's side, and braced off. This was done so quickly that the boat swerved scarcely an inch from its course.

Creole Charley came up spouting water. He clambered back on deck, picked up an extra pole, and again took his place in the line.

When the boat was finally pushed through the rapids Captain Billy again sent the men ashore for a rest period. While Micky was gathering up the fragments of the feast, he couldn't resist the temptation to tease Creole Charley.

"Next time you see a big fish, try spearin' him with your pole. Don't go tryin' again to catch him with your two hands."

"I'll be flyblowed if it ever happened to me before," said Creole Charley humbly. "Why, I was usin' the same pole I pushed all the way the last voyage. When we went up through Middle Chute at the Falls last year, you know I helped hold 'er steady through a channel so narrow a fish couldn't agot through without scrapin' off half his scales."

"You'll be flyblowed sure 'nough," added the Mocker with contagious good humor, "if you're not more careful in setting your pole firm. We'd have lost *Half Moon* sure as shootin' if Captain Billy hadn't set his alligator-horse strength quick as a flash on your side o' the boat."

Micky added with a chuckle, "A bullfrog could take a lesson in quick divin' from you, Creole Charley."

It was when the *Half Moon* reached the Grand Chain that the going became next to impossible. Captain Billy ordered the cordelle out, and sent his men ashore to drag the boat forward with brute strength. Mike was stationed at the prow, with his pole thrown wide to brace off the boat so that it would not nose into the shallow water and go aground.

The cordelle men, with Micky in the lead, toiled over shifting gravel. They stumbled over shale rock, and tangled their feet among stunted willow sprouts. But whatever the hazard or the obstruction, the *Half Moon* went steadily forward.

At times the crewmen grumbled. Some of them fought fatigue and ague. But they all carried on.

Navigating a keelboat against so powerful a current, beset with a thousand obstacles on every side, seemed a romantic adventure to Mike. Others might think the Mississippi a luring siren and a heartless harpy, but to young Mike she was a glamorous, lovely lady. She was stubborn and full of surprises, but his heart was hers. She demanded every ounce of his muscular prowess. She baffled his will as nothing else ever had. She was ten times as explosive as the worst plug-ugly river bully. But Mike took ten times more satisfaction in having his way against her. Deep down in his soul Mike knew that sailing the Mississippi was the life for him. Nothing else mattered.

After weeks of grimy toil and struggle, the *Half Moon* tied up at Shippingport. The cargo had to be portaged before the boat could be navigated over the Falls.

Here again Mike found the pack work to his liking. His muscles cried out for something really hard to do. Willingly he shouldered twice the load of coffee and molasses that the other crewmen carried. He toted it without seeming effort up the long path to the dock at Louisville. The two long miles seemed but twenty or thirty paces, and he helped carry a downstream cargo back. With a bag of corn meal riding lightly on his shoulder and a smoked ham under his arm, he strode along whistling a merry tune.

The professional pilots looked hard at Mike and then at Captain Billy. "What sort o' young alligator-horse you got here?" they asked incredulously.

"He's young Mike Fink," said Captain Billy proudly. "Mike can outwork and outfight any man ever seen on the river. Why, he can whip his weight in wildcats!"

"You're right. We see about all the boatmen in the world in action, an' we've never set eyes on anything near his equal."

Weeks later when young Mike strode into the Sign of the Catfish, Ephraim Jones looked him over for a full minute before he recognized him. "Well, if my eyes don't lie," he drawled, reaching out his hand, "you're Mike. Say, one voyage down the river has made a sure 'nough alligator-horse out o' you. Drat my chilblains, you've feathered out good around the cheeks an' gills."

Mike grinned. "An' how's Uncle Charley gettin' on?"

"Fine as a fiddle-de-dee." Ephraim was smiling, too. "Rovin' Charley is due here any minute now. He comes in every night to ask if I've heard anything new about you. And nearly every day I pick up some new tale o' wonder. What you been doin' anyhow, you young riproarer, to start such a smoke? You're the most talked-of boatman on the entire river. Nobody less than a Davy Crockett or a Dan'l Boone can hold a candle to you."

"Shouldn't be surprised there must be some mistake," said Mike, ignoring the compliment. "These rivermen must be gettin' me mixed up with some other fellow."

Ephraim gave Mike a hug. "You may as well own up to everything. I knowed right away when I see you lay Micky Thunderbolt out cold and drag him through that door by the heels that you was a miracle man."

"You say Uncle Charley is due here now?" asked Mike, growing anxious.

"Jes' keep your shirt on a minute or two longer, young fightin' cock. He'll be here without fail."

"Well, then set me up some victuals. I feel as hollow as an ol' hollow log."

6.   The Happiest Man Alive

"Well, I'll be flyblowed if here's not my long-lost darlin'," roared Roving Charley as he bounced into the tavern and threw his arms around Mike. "What are all these wild tales I been hearin' 'bout you? One Captain brings word that you carry a thunderbolt in each fist. Whoever you swing at you hit, and whoever you hit you lay out cold. Why, the way I hear it, you musta crumpled the knees of every cock-a-doodle river bully all the way down to Natchez-under-the-Hill an' back."

"An' jes' to think, Mike," chortled Ephraim, no longer able to keep quiet, "your Uncle Charley wouldn't at first believe you knocked down an' dragged out the mighty Micky Thunderbolt."

"After all I been hearin', I'll believe anything. Why, they say you done better at that beef raffle down in Kentuck than the best Dan'l Boone an' Davy Crockett ever done, put together. An' at the Falls portage, they saw you totin' a barrel o' molasses on each shoulder an' a bag o' Java coffee under each arm. They say you carried four times as much as the best riverman ever carried, an' besides you was awhistlin' fit to kill, while you worked."

Young Mike shrugged his shoulders and winked at Ephraim. "You're old enough, Uncle Charley, to know the way rivermen hatch out tall tales. . . . By the way, how you been doin' with your trappin'?"

"Not too bad. I got enough pelts to reach a mile or more, if you laid 'em down side by side."

"Well then, let's get going. I'll help you carry them downtown to market in your canoe. . . . So long, Ephraim. We'll be seein' you again."

Mike examined the peltry. "Why, you got next to a fortune here!"

"But tell me, lad, what have you learned while you been away?"

Mike lifted his chest and chin. "I learned one thing: For the rest of my life I'm goin' to be a keelboat captain."

Roving Charley grinned, and his eyes sparkled. "This don't astonish me none. If half the tales about you are true, I know you're a natural sailorman."

"I've not done too much, but I've been lucky in most everything I've tried. I'm hopin' you don't think I'm too young to be a keelboat captain right away. You see, I've saved all my wages, an' besides, Micky's shared half the money he's made layin' bets on me. I have enough money to make a big down payment on the *Half Moon*. Captain Billy wants to sell out. He's had his fill of the river, and wants to settle down on a home-stead at the mouth of the Marietta River."

"Why, this is a happy surprise!" Uncle Charley began to pace back and forth in front of his cabin door. "This is sure a good idea, that is if —"

Mike cut him short. "What I'm wondering is this: If —"

"Don't you interrupt me, lad. I got an idea that my peltry will pay all you lack on the *Half Moon*."

"I'll pay you back every cent. This solves everything!"

Uncle Charley started dancing a jig. "Oh no, it don't. I got to give you somethin' besides. . . . Yes, I got it. I'll jes' turn in an' pay for a new sail. Then when you happen to have a fair wind, you can think o' your Uncle Charley."

Mike grasped Roving Charley's hand. "I don't know how to thank you for all you're doing. Nothing could please me more."

"And when I'm atrampin' the woods, runnin' my string o' traps, or paddlin' my canoe, I can dream o' you an' your happy life."

Mike hurried back to the river and made a deal with Captain Billy for the purchase of his boat. He also hired all the crewmen he knew so well.

Thus Mike Fink became the youngest keelboat captain ever to sail the Inland Waterway from Pittsburgh to New Orleans. Before starting his first voyage Mike had Roving Charley's new sail reefed to the mast, and a new name across the bow of his boat: Light Foot.

The morning young Captain Mike ordered his *Light Foot* out on the rolling current, he was the happiest man alive. The scent of wild flowers was in the air and the songs of a thousand

birds. But Captain Mike and his men saw and heard little that went on about them.

The crewmen were staring wide-eyed at their powerful young master, standing astride the tiller. Mike was grinning from ear to ear. All he wished for had come true. His steady feet were planted on the deck of his own boat. His eyes were on the beckoning river. She was in one of her flirting moods, happy and carefree, but he was studying her hidden secrets, thinking only of the safety of his boat and cargo.

Day after day the sun shone warm, and the river smiled upon Mike's maiden voyage. The crewmen were happy, too. They worshiped the sturdy lad at the tiller.

"What a man!" said Micky under his breath. "He never needs to be told a thing twice."

The Mocker's eyes twinkled. "That's right. What he sees once, he always remembers."

"Look at the way he handles that heavy sweep," replied Micky. "You'd think he'd been at it all his life."

The Mocker picked up his fiddle, crossed his legs and teetered his toe in time with the melody.

> Oh, our ship's makin' speed;
> We're far in the lead
> Of the flat that we started behind;
> For the barge we're too fast,
> The long-horn we've passed;
> We're out ahead on the wings o' the wind.

He kept up his chanting till he was tired, and then called to Creole Charley and Old Faithful. They did a merry jig and the buck and wing.

When Captain Mike had brought them over the Falls without the slightest mishap, the crewmen were really surprised.

"Why, even Captain Billy, after years at the sweep, couldn't have done a slicker job," said the Mocker.

Micky added, "I'll put you up against anybody on the river when it comes to navigatin' a keelboat, yes, an' I'll win my bet."

The wind caught hold of the sail and sent *Light Foot* tripping forward. The Mocker laid his fiddle across his knees and looked up at Mike. "Don't suppose, Cap'n, you heard of the tragedy that happened here at Indian Chute a few months before you started sailin'."

"Tell me about it," said Mike.

"A long-horn named the *Beaver* was navigatin' the Falls with Cap'n Tommy Hartley mannin' the sweep. The boat was dancin' at a merry clip down the chute when, believe it or not, a bullet crashed through Cap'n Tommy's right shoulder. The Cap'n lost his hold on the tiller, an' the *Beaver* was ground to kindlin' wood. The craft was carryin' a cargo of bacon and salt pork, an' the skulkin' outlaws picked up the few barrels that were not torn to pieces."

"I heard tell," added Micky, "that the crime might o' been done by a gang o' cutthroats that are holed up at Cave-in-Rock. Leastwise it looks mighty suspicious it was them."

Captain Mike stepped astride the tiller to relax his arms, and grinned.

"You'll have to keep your eyes peeled for outlaws while I watch the current."

"But don't think we're afraid o' no outlaws," said Micky, lifting his chin. "They'll be a sorry lot that attacks us."

* * *

An hour later, when *Light Foot* pulled up alongside a clumsy flat that was carrying an emigrant family and all their earthly possessions, the Mocker began asking foolish questions.

"Come far, stranger?"

The skinny little weather-beaten man sniffed, and then smiled. "Seems only a few miles to me, but my old woman an' the kids think it's been halfway round the world."

"Where you headed for?"

"Downstream," the wife answered in dry humor.

"Got your homestead located yet?"

"Say, what you think Providence is for," replied the man, "but to lean on in a time like this?"

Micky looked on in glee until the emigrant and his wife had silenced the Mocker. By this time *Light Foot* was far ahead of the flat. "You old smarty!" said Micky. "Why didn't you ask the stranger if his mother-in-law is cross-eyed an' whether his bay nag's got the glanders?"

The emigrant in the next flat they passed asked the questions. To make up for his previous failure, the Mocker answered for the entire crew.

"Where you fellers hail from?" asked the round-shouldered, long-nosed emigrant.

The Mocker pretended to be bored. "From home, where you s'pose?"

"Where's that?"

"Wherever we hang up our coonskin caps."

"Where you headed for?"

"We're all curious to find where the river ends."

"You happen to know where's a good place for me an' my family to take up a homestead?"

"By the clumsy way you're navigatin' I allow you'll soon strike a snag or drift into a wooden island or get stranded on a sand bar. Whenever some calamity o'ertakes you, stranger, my advice to you is this: Put your question to the first muskrat you happen to meet. Then hire the muskrat to tow you an' your traps ashore. Sooner than you can say 'Scat!' where your feet touch solid ground will be home-sweet-home to you all."

The rotund wife shouted after the advancing *Light Foot:* "You think you're mighty smart! You're the kind o' slicker I wouldn't even wipe my feet on. . . ."

Despite all this nonsense, Captain Mike kept his eyes glued to the river, and the tiller moving back and forth. He enjoyed nonsense as much as anybody, and was glad his men were happy.

Later when *Light Foot* tied up at Henderson Landing, Barney Ogle, keeper of the Black Bear, told Mike and his men he was sure a band of outlaws were operating out of Cave-in-Rock. This was a natural cave in a cliff of rock twenty-five miles further downstream, on the Indiana side of the river.

"What makes you think so?" asked Mike.

"A few days ago an Injun canoe stopped here," said Ogle. "A shifty-eyed slicker was in command. His reddish-brown hair was plastered down with b'ar grease, and his tongue was oilier'n coon fat. He was dressed out in plaid store clothes 'at fitted him like skin to a rabbit. He had two men dressed in woodsmen's buckskin, an' not as rivermen. They had shifty eyes, and hard faces. There was also a dog-in-manger fellow with a rifle cradled across his forearm, an' a long knife danglin' from his belt. They said they had come to trade me out of a barrel o' corn meal, an' a bushel o' salt. But the way they was asquintin' around an' stickin' their noses into everything, I didn't trust them an inch out o' my sight."

"And did you trade with them?" asked Mike.

"They tried to trade me a woman's gold ring, an' then a woman's breastpin. But I told 'em it was hard money with me or nothin'. An' they finally came across."

Mike was letting all this sink in. "But what makes you so certain they're outlaws?"

"Mebbe I'm o'erreachin' myself to tell you all this," said Ogle with a nervous twitch of his shoulders, "but I've knowed two or three o' your crewmen for several years. I had several honest deals with Captain Billy on his way up an' down the river. So I'm takin' a wild shot and givin' you good an' fair warnin'."

"You don't need to be afraid for us," said Mike.

"Well, you see, after the slickers had gone, I had plenty o' time to chew my cud and think things over. An' I decided, if I was a slicker like that Judas-haired feller, the only reason I'd start a tavern in Cave-in-Rock would be to waylay an' rob — yes, an' kill — honest sailors."

Mike paid careful attention to every word. "What you say, Ogle, sounds reasonable."

"Well, I wasn't satisfied till I went to see for myself what was goin' on. So I took my bark canoe an' my trusty Provider, an' a snack to eat. I managed it so I paddled the last five or six knots under cover o' darkness. When early dawn came, I beached my canoe at the mouth of a creek, in a clump o' willows. I laid over all day, and saw the slickers paddle up and down along each bank of the river, to make sure no one was spyin' on Cave-in-Rock. With Provider handy, I laid low an' made sure they didn't see me.

"Then when it was dark again I crawled out, an' picked my way through the tangle of woods, an' climbed the ledge o' limestone rock overlookin' the openin' to the cave. When the moon came up, I could see a long way up an' down the river. I found also that my hiding place was bein' used by someone durin' the day as a lookout. A bower o' elm brush an' a long rifle cached under a piece o' sailcloth was all the evidence I needed.

"I could see men busy as beavers carryin' things up from the river an' takin' them inside the cave. Looked as if they was cachin' the cargo o' some flat they'd waylaid.

"While the moon was still high, I hurried back to my canoe, an' I'm tellin' you I wasn't a minute too soon. A skulkin' guard had located my canoe and was searchin' for my paddle. I brought Provider to my shoulder, but before I could crook my trigger finger, the man leaped behind a tree and fled.

"An' believe me, I pushed that canoe out o' them willows like a scared deer, an' rowed like mad across the river an' upstream. At early dawn I again beached my canoe, and remained under cover all day. This time when darkness fell I pushed off upstream, an' didn't stop till I was safe here at home."

"You've done us a good turn," said Mike, grasping Ogle's hand. "We'll be on the lookout for more information, an' when we return we'll let you know what we find out."

Next day the men strained their eyes as they glided past Cave-in-Rock. Micky was at the tiller and Mike had his Bang All handy. He was sure he saw a man's head slowly lift above the lookout bower and then slowly lower out of sight.

Nailed to a water-oak tree they saw a sign painted in large red letters, THE BOATMAN'S HAVEN.

A man quickly stepped down to the dock and called out: "Better stop an' see one o' the great Wonders o' the World. This natural cave is the Greatest Wonder West of Pittsburgh!"

Mike shouted back, "How's business?"

"Fine," answered the man. "Why not drop in for a social visit? Besides showing the wonders of the cave, we serve the best victuals an' offer the best lodging anywhere on the river."

"What's your name?" shouted Mike, sending the echoes flying.

"It's tacked up here on this tree for all to read."

"I mean your landlord's name."

"John Smith, from Philadelphia. . . . And what's your captain's name?"

Quick as a flash Mike bellowed, "John Smith, Jr., from Boston."

"We must be kinfolk," shouted the man. "Now you'll have to stop till we can figure out our relation."

"Thank you so much, but we've other fish to fry to-day. . . ."

When they were out of earshot of the cave, Mocker picked up his fiddle and chanted:

> Steer clear of the river whenever you can,
> She's a heartless maiden since time began;
> Every turn of her feet is filled with deceit,
> She's a siren, a vixen, an uncommon cheat;
> Steer clear of the river, wherever you go;
> The firm earth's your friend, the river your foe.

"Another crack out o' you," snarled Micky, "an I'll boot you, fiddle an' all, off this boat."

Mike laughed. "Don't forget that a change is the spice o' life."

The weather continued perfect, and Mike and his men were kept busy thinking up ways to entertain each other. Mike loved practical jokes. One day he asked Micky to take a turn at the tiller, so he could do a little shooting.

"See them young pigs friskin' round their mother yonder, under that sycamore?" he said, pointing with his forefinger. "Every one o' them has got his owner's brand cut in his ear. Even you, Mocker, should be able to see that. What'll you bet me I can't put my brand on tother end o' them, without in the least injurin' their health an' happiness?" When Mocker hesitated, Mike added with a gruff boom, "I'll bet any of you a week's wages I can do it with Bang All. Come on now, why don't you speak up?"

"You know, Captain Mike," answered the Mocker, "you've not missed the bull's-eye since I've knowed you, an' you're not likely to miss now."

Without more ado, Mike drew back his foot, and lifted Bang All into position and crooked his trigger finger. Fifty yards away, a small pig jumped and squealed.

Mike grinned. "What did I tell you! I cut his tail off slick and clean as a barber's razor." He rammed home another bullet. "What'll you bet I can't do the same thing to each an' every pig?"

"We're only bettin' you'll hit everything you aim at," said Micky in deep admiration. "If you want to lay a bet, ask the emigrant on this flat we're passin'."

"What'll you bet me, stranger," Mike boomed, "that I can't shoot the tail feathers off one o' them pigs, without injurin' the pig in any other way?"

"You must be young Captain Mike Fink," answered the man. "I been hearin' a hundred times how pizen you are with Bang All. No, I'm not bettin'."

"Well, stranger, don't look at me, then." Captain Mike sifted powder in his pan. "If you won't pay your admission, then you're not entitled to a ringside seat at this show."

A second pig jumped and squealed, and a second pigtail fell to the ground. This happened a third and a fourth time. The continuing gunfire brought the homesteader's wife to the river-bank in a hurry. She brandished her husband's rifle. "What you up to, you scurvy boatman?" she shouted in a harsh nasal twang. "For twopence I'd shoot a hole through your liver an' let the sun in to shame your wicked heart."

Mike removed his cap and curtsied. "Pardon me, my good woman. I mean no harm in the world. I was just hoping you'd come out so I could present you with fresh meat for a kettle o' pigtail soup."

"You can't fool me none," shrieked the woman. "You're Mike Fink all right, and a scoundrel to boot. I know all about your slick thievin' ways."

"You got me entirely wrong," boomed Mike. "Of course I like a practical joke, but I never have stolen a penny from any homesteader. It just happens it's more fun not to steal. Bang All keeps me an' my men supplied with all the wild meat we can eat. When we crave pork, we barter venison or b'ar steak or wild turkey."

"You can't salve my wounds with any o' your slick palaver," snorted the woman. "An' if ever again I ketch you shootin' up any more o' my pigs, I'll put a bullet hole through you, you villain, if it's the last thing I ever do."

"Sorry, my good woman," shouted Mike as the boat drifted out of earshot. "It won't happen again."

A minute later Mike said, thinking aloud, "I wonder who's been sowin' thistle seed in my tracks, an' scatterin' pizen tales about me."

"Could be them rascals down at Cave-in-Rock," said the Mocker. Then to restore good cheer, he began to chant:

> I was purty badly whipped — so was Davy Crockett.
> I looked around an' found my head a-missin';
> He had shot off my head, an' I had swallowed hisn.
> Then we did agree to let each other be,
> I was too much for him, an' he was too much for me.

By the time Mocker had finished, everybody was laughing.

Weeks later at Natchez-under-the-Hill Mike and Micky met an outfit that aroused their suspicion. The two men in charge of the flat were dressed in woodsmen's buckskin, and didn't act like rivermen. They had shifty eyes and sharp lean faces. One had a deep scar across his left cheek and the other a gash over his right temple. Each carried a brace of horse pistols and a pearl-handled long knife dangling from his braided rattlesnake belt. Each wore a broad-brimmed felt hat over his eyes, and appeared to be haunted by some fear.

"These must be the freebooters from Cave-in-Rock that Ogle told us about," said Mike in a whisper.

Their cargo consisted of three or four sets of frontier emigrant goods.

"How about strikin' up some sort o' trade?" Mike asked them.

"We're not interested in anything but hard money," answered the taller man, casting a quick sidelong glance. "We're heelin' it back home over the Natchez Trace, an' we can't carry anything heavier than silver."

"How you pricin' that pile o' ginseng?" asked Mike.

"You'll be surprised. You can have it for half the warehouse price."

"How many pounds you got?"

The man answered glibly, "Fifty-nine and six ounces."

"If you'll accept the weight o' my balance scales," said Mike, "I'll take all you got."

"I'll not have any man alive question my weights," snarled the man.

Mike smiled. "An' I never buy anything without checkin' the weight."

The shorter man had a woman's watch and breastpin he wanted to sell cheap. This only deepened Mike's and Micky's suspicion.

After two days of bartering Mike had his downstream cargo disposed of and his upstream cargo loaded. He and his men were just turning in for the night when a stranger came on deck, and asked with jaunty ease if he could hire passage to Louisville.

Mike looked the stranger over while the man kept his shifty eyes shaded behind the brim of his beaver hat. His plaid suit of store clothes fitted snug as a rabbit's skin, and his square-toed cowskin boots shone like mirrors. There wasn't one thing about the smart-mannered stranger that Mike liked.

"How much you expectin' to pay?" asked Mike coolly.

"Oh, say three times as much as you charge for twice my weight of ordinary freight." The stranger grinned. "That ought to be enough to make even a keelboat captain happy."

"An' what about the victuals?"

"Any price you think right will suit me fine."

"What's your name?"

For a fleeting second the stranger looked Mike straight in the eye. "Talbot is my name. It's like this: My mother up in Louisville is badly ailing, and wants very much to see me before she passes on. I'm told your *Light Foot*'s the fastest keelboat afloat; that's why I'll pay you handsomely for my passage."

All this sounded a bit sentimental coming from such a slicker, but Mike thought there was one chance in a thousand that he might be telling the truth. "If you're willin' to share our cabin an' our coarse food, Mr. Talbot, I'll take you."

The stranger pulled out a fistful of hard money. "Thank you. Here's my fare."

"Follow me," said Mike, "an' don't stub your toe on this cleated companionway, or batter your beaver hat on this overhead timber. Here you are. Take this bunk furtherest from the hatch." He paused and grinned. "An' may the Good Lord pity you, if you're a light sleeper, in this menagerie o' wild varmints!"

This time Mike proved an easy mark, for Talbot was not only a light sleeper: he was light-fingered to boot. The men were scarcely asleep when he went through their pockets. Mike was even robbed of the fare Talbot had just paid! Without being heard, Talbot slipped out through the hatch, leaving it unlatched.

Later in the night when Mike's first sound sleep had lightened he heard a noise at the hatch. It was the Cave-in-Rock gang, bent on shackling Mike and his crew, and taking *Light Foot* under their own command.

Mike quickly aroused his men, and the next minute the cabin was an inferno of slugging and clawing, grunting and gouging, howling and biting. Things were twenty times fiercer than two packs of wildcats in a death struggle.

When at last the fight ended, each sturdy crewman had his gangster in hand. Mike carried each of the attackers up on deck, and tossed his limp body to the wharf. Only the slicker Talbot escaped without injury. He had neither a scratch on his person nor a dent in his immaculate beaver hat.

"This time the laugh's on me," Mike chuckled hoarsely. "Any fool should have known at first sight that this slicker Talbot was the very same crook Ogle told us about weeks ago."

Before the first sign of earliest dawn, *Light Foot* had begun her upstream voyage. Mike was at the tiller, grinning from ear to ear. "Them Cave-in-Rock crooks'll sure have a time explainin' away their sorry plight." His face grew serious. "But we'll lay in a good supply of war clubs an' horse pistols. Next time a gang o' bullies board us, we'll pile 'em up on the pier like bags o' salt."

7. Who's Afeard of a Knife or a Bullet or Two?

On the upstream voyage everything went forward as usual until they tied *Light Foot* up at the Louisville dock. There they found Constable Cassady awaiting them, with a warrant for Captain Mike's arrest.

In confidence, the constable told them, "It's like this, the warrant was sworn out by a gang o' scalawags that are jealous o' your prowess on the river. They've been pesterin' us around the courthouse for weeks awaitin' your return."

Captain Mike was astonished. "What's this all about?"

"It's all a parcel of lies fur as I can make out."

"What am I charged with?"

"You're charged first with shootin' Squire Doolittle's seven shoats, and further with the willful and malicious intent of transportin' them to the deck o' your *Light Foot*. All this is supposed to have transpired on the night o' the seventeenth o' September last. Previous to this date, the Squire's wife swears she caught you red-handed in the act o' shootin' the seven tails off the same seven pigs. She heard you say with her own ears that you were placin' your bloody brand on them hogs. She alleges further that she clearly saw the name *Light Foot* painted out clear in big letters across the prow o' yer keelboat."

Captain Mike laughed, "I did shoot the tails off her pigs, Cassady. This I did in jest to keep my crew in a good humor. But when it comes to killin' the shoats, that's a barefaced lie."

"I'm sure it's a lie," agreed the constable. "But you haven't heard the half of it yet. It's further charged that on the afternoon of November fifteenth last, you willfully and with malicious intent cheated Farmer Collins out o' three o' his choicest spring lambs."

Captain Mike's face turned crimson with rage. "You don't say!" he exclaimed. "Why, truth is that *Light Foot* was down at Point Chicot that very day. Reason I remember the date is that I was bartering salt for cane sirup, and later the sirup molded before I could dispose of it."

"I'm sure you speak nothing but the truth," purred the constable. "But listen till I'm finished. It's here further charged that on the said fifteenth day o' November last, you an' your crewman, Micky Thunderbolt, landed in your yawl below Farmer Collins's pasture lot with a bladder of Scotch snuff you'd filched from your entrusted cargo. An' while said Farmer Collins was busy in his barn shuckin' nubbins, you an' Micky caught each o' the said lambs, an' with malicious intent rubbed Scotch snuff in each o' their several noses an' faces an' eyes. Then, while you,

Captain Mike, stood guard, Micky ran to find Farmer Collins to tell him somethin' terrific had befallen his flock.

"Farmer Collins found his three lambs performin' as if possessed o' the seven devils. They were jumpin' stiff-legged as if trying to hop over the moon, rubbin' their eyes out on the sod, and snortin' like Gabriel's last trump o' doom.

"It's further charged that you, Captain Mike, asked the astonished farmer if he knowed what was the matter with his sheep. The farmer answered he was surprised anything was the matter with them. You told him a pestilence known as 'murrain' was ragin' up an' down the river, and that this plague was the most contagious disease ever let loose in this world among sheep. You made him believe that unless he killed these three lambs instantly, the disease would spread an' he would lose his entire flock. The farmer moaned that his long rifle was at Gunsmith Chamberlain's for repair, an' that even if he had his gun he had not the heart to kill his pets. It is then alleged that you agreed to help Farmer Collins out. If he'd give you a gallon of his choicest peach brandy, you'd attend to the little matter right away. While Micky went with Farmer Collins to fetch the jug o' peach brandy, you dispatched the three lambs with Bang All, an' tossed their carcasses into the river so the imagined disease wouldn't spread."

"The villains!" snorted Captain Mike, purple with rage.

"But this is not all. After darkness fell, you an' Micky fished the three lambs out o' the shallow water where you'd thrown them. You an' your crewmen then had more mutton and peach-brandy sauce than you could eat."

"But what makes Farmer Collins believe these lies?" asked Captain Mike.

"Farmer Collins alleges," continued the constable in even tones, "that he asked said riverman his name. You answered him, 'I'm the one and only Captain Mike Fink. Can't you see I'm half alligator an' half horse? This red feather in my cap means I've whipped every crowin' bully along all the two thousand miles o' runnin' water from Pittsburgh to New Orleans. I can outhop, outskip, outjump, outfight every other fresh-water roarer in the universe!'"

"It doesn't stand to reason I'd reveal my name after doing such a rascally deed," growled Mike in disgust. "Even a child can see that."

"This's jes' what I been sayin' to myself. An' after considerin' the matter for a long time, I've concluded the scalawags that brought these charges musta rigged out one of their thieves as your double. For several months past I been hearing about many supposedly unmanly deeds o' yours. An' unless I'm badly mistaken, somebody has been hidin' behind your personality an' has been doing these depredations himself."

Captain Mike was getting madder every minute. "Just wait till I get my claws on the villain!"

"Not quite so fast," said the constable. "Stop a minute longer while I finish. As I have said, I got here the warrant for your arrest. A reward of a hundred Spanish dollars has been offered on your head, an' that's a lot of money in anybody's language. You know me well enough, Captain Mike, to believe I'm your true friend. You also must know I'm in need of a little extra hard money. Now one way you can get even with the scoundrels is to help me collect the offered reward. I'll pledge my honor you'll be found entirely innocent of all these trumped-up charges."

Captain Mike weighed the matter. "How many of the gang-sters are there?" he asked.

"Seventeen that I know about, an' a lot o' extra hangers-on."

"Have you noticed a lank, shifty-eyed desperado?" asked Captain Mike. "He has a deep scar across his left cheek, and a jerk in his left foot like a spring-halted nag, and he always has a brace of horse pistols and a pearl-handled long knife dangling from his braided alligator belt."

The constable opened his eyes in surprise. "You've described the very man who's leader o' the posse. He signed the warrant as Thomas Brown."

"I begin to smell a rat," snarled Captain Mike. "I met this very fine gentleman some months ago, disposing of what looked mighty like a stolen cargo, down at Natchez-under-the-Hill. Unless I'm badly mistaken he's one of the gang of outlaws now operating out o' Cave-in-Rock."

"It wouldn't surprise me none if you're right," agreed the constable. "Jes' come along with me up to the court house, an' I'll get you acquitted for lack o' evidence."

"That's easy enough to say, Constable," said Captain Mike, still undecided. "If these were honest men, I'd go with you in a minute. If there was any honor among their gang, I'd be glad to agree to whip 'em one by one, fast as they could step up to me. You may not know it, Constable, but these are the kind that put a knife or a bullet in your back when you least expect it."

"You don't mean to tell me you're scared to go," said the constable in surprise.

"I'm not afraid of any man alive," said Mike firmly. "You know I've whipped every crowing bully I've met up and down the river, and I'm proud I've never had to disfigure or kill any of them. But this fight is different. It's not an honest rough-and-tumble tussle with no holds barred and may the best man win. This is skulking, dishonest, premeditated murder."

"Aren't you imagining things?"

"These gangsters know me, and I once tarred and feathered them. My merry men and I have crossed their trail before. They're scared we'll some day spoil their fun, and so they want to rid the river of our interference. They won't stop at anything to get me!"

"Well, now's as good a time as any to settle the score," urged the constable.

"You seem to forget that I'm a riverman. I don't feel at home any place but in my boat. I'd rather wait and come to grips with those crooks sometime when they're not expecting me."

The constable seemed very sad. "If you only knowed how much my old woman and the children need the reward money, Captain Mike," he complained, "you wouldn't fail me this time."

"Well, old friend, since you put it this way, I'll take a chance. But, I'll go only under one condition. You send a long-coupled wagon and two good ox teams to the riverbank here, and me and my men'll load our yawl on the wheels. We'll all climb into the yawl, armed to the teeth, and defy the gangsters to attack us."

"Agreed," the constable said, relieved. "I'll be settin' out this very minute before you have time to change your mind."

While the pudgy constable clambered up the steep hill into the town, Captain Mike and his men planned their strategy.

It was high noon when heavy oxen came lumbering very slowly up the hill at Third Street. Mike stood in the stern of his yawl with Bang All draped alertly across the crook in his arm. His crewmen were seated around the sides of the yawl, each with his gun in one hand and in the other his long iron-tipped pole "tossed," ready for instant action.

"This is the first aquatic excursion on land I ever experienced," drawled the Mocker.

Micky was in high spirits. "Bless me, this is more fun than a river full o' floatin' islands at the crest o' the spring freshet," he cackled.

The yawl swayed and rocked atop the wagon.

"My merry men," boomed Captain Mike, "I've only this to say to you all. We're now on our way to meet a gang o' desperate men. Each o' you has his long knife and his horse pistol spoiling for action. Today you're my personal bodyguard, and you must keep on the alert constantly. Keep me surrounded at all times, and keep every man in the crowd covered."

With jaw set, Micky said grimly: "You can trust me, Captain Mike. If anybody starts gettin' funny, we'll turn his innards out'ards instanter."

As the lumbering oxen brought the bouncing yawl to the brow of the hill, Mike suddenly changed his mind. Without warning he commanded, "Set poles!" In astonishment the men obeyed. Then, before they had time to comprehend what was happening, Captain Mike shouted, "Back her!" Within the second, the men threw their weight on the poles. The oxen had not been trained to walk backwards. They braced themselves, and had to be dragged down the hillside. Their scraping hoofs set the loose rocks rolling. They bellowed in fear, but Mike's booming voice drowned out all other sounds.

"It's the first time in yer life ye ever backed water," moaned Micky. "Whatever's got into ye, Captain Mike?"

"Hold your tongue!" commanded Captain Mike firmly. "Do as you're told!"

When the yawl again reached the riverbank, Captain Mike commanded: "Set poles! Hold 'er fast!"

While the bewildered oxen and the men stood frozen in their places Captain Mike took plenty of time to turn several different matters over in his mind. After a prolonged silence, he said: "I want all you men to understand I'm not scared. The thing of it is, I don't want to get any of you murdered unless it's necessary."

Micky was as eager as a fighting cock. "Who's afeard of a knife or a bullet or two?" he said. "A good scuffle is what we're all spoiling for."

"What I want you all to understand is that this is not a good or honest fight," said Captain Mike in a quiet voice. "A gang o' cutthroats and gangsters are lying in wait for us. They'll never strike us when we're looking their way. They'll stick us in the back as they did Squire Doolittle's shoats. Knowing this, if you all still want to go with me, I'll order the oxen up the hill again."

"Of course we all want to see you through," shouted the Mocker.

Micky grinned. "Only give us your orders," he added, "an' we'll go through hell an' high water with you, Captain Mike."

"Toss your poles, my merry men, and cock your pistols," shouted Captain Mike. "Ox drivers, goad your teams forward."

When the strange equipage arrived in front of the courthouse, the waiting crowd stared in wonder. Captain Mike and his men leaped to the ground and in swinging stride walked in close formation into the courtroom. Each crewman carried his knife unsheathed in one hand and his horse pistol cocked in the other. They kept Captain Mike surrounded at all times, and their fiery eyes covered every person present.

The witnesses were waiting, ready to appear in their turn. Mrs. Doolittle took the stand first. After she had given her testimony, Captain Mike addressed the court: "Your Honor, Mr. Judge, I'd like to act as my own counsel."

"Your petition is granted," replied the amused judge, bringing his cane down across the table with a thump.

"Mrs. Doolittle," boomed Captain Mike, "you were just saying you remember the day I shot the seven tails off your seven little pigs."

"Who could ever forget such a disgraceful scene?"

"You say further that you saw me, on the night o' September seventeen last, kill your seven shoats and carry them aboard my *Light Foot*."

"I should say I do."

"How did you say I killed the pigs?"

"You slashed their throats with yer long knife."

"Was the moon shining or was it dark?"

"I don't remember exactly."

"Try hard to think."

After a prolonged silence, Mrs. Doolittle said, "The moon must have been shining. How else could I have seen you?"

"There's where you're wrong, Mrs. Doolittle. You wonder how I happen to remember so well that particular night. Well, it's like this. Me and my merry men were pulling *Light Foot* up on the sandy beach at Hurricane Island to calk a leak in her keel with tar, and we all know there was no moon. Mr. Judge, it's easy for you to refer to your own almanac for the truth."

While the judge convinced himself that this particular date fell in the dark of the moon, Captain Mike said to Mrs. Doolittle, "Sometimes I like mischief, and play a practical joke, but I promise you I got none of your pigs' blood on my hands."

Suddenly the opposition lawyer was aware of the point of a long knife at his ribs. "Mr. Judge!" he shrieked. "I have a dozen other indictments and witnesses."

Captain Mike toyed with the trigger of his gun. "With your permission, Mr. Judge," he said, rising, "I'll come back another day to answer the remainder of these trumped-up charges."

The judge arose quickly. "Charges unfounded. Court's adjourned," he said as he brought his loaded cane down with a thump.

Captain Mike's crewmen, forming a revolving wheel of hot and cold steel around their leader, quickly forced their way through the angry crowd to the waiting yawl. Captain Mike took his place at the stern, his Bang All cocked and primed, while his men, with poles "tossed" and horse pistols handy, eyed every scowling gangster out of countenance.

As the oxen moved, Micky cackled in glee, "We're safe as a porcupine with all his quills on end."

The yawl tossed and pitched as the oxen lumbered slowly down the hill.

"Don't relax your vigilance for a second," trumpeted Captain Mike.

When at last they were aboard *Light Foot*, Captain Mike took his place at the sweep, and said in a relieved tone of voice: "We're mighty lucky to slip out o' the jaws of that b'ar trap, without springin' it. But you can bet your bottom dollar the next time Constable Cassady wants to collect another reward, he'll have to pick on a fightin' cock of another feather."

Suddenly Captain Mike's face was aglow, and he boomed out joyously: "To your stations, my merry men! Cast off the bow-lines! Set your oars! We're hittin' for the rolling tide where no gangster dares show his face above water."

8. Fighting Outlaws

A year later Mike and his men were working their way downstream not far from Cave-in-Rock. The current was slow and the men at the oars were hot and bothered. Mike flicked the sweat from his forehead with his forefinger. "This air hasn't any more life than a dead snappin' turtle," he mumbled. "The weather is crafty. Looks like it's brewin' a mighty bad storm."

The Mocker blew the dripping sweat from his upper lip. "Hear that rumble o' thunder. She sounds like an old pealer's on our tail."

The first wind came in spiteful gusts. A minute or two later the trees began creaking and swaying. Suddenly the river was rougher than an alligator's back. There was a blinding, deafening crash of lightning, and the storm was upon them. The heavens opened wide, and down came the rain and hail in blinding gusty sheets, one after another. The men couldn't see where the rain left off and the river began.

Mike set the cadence for the oars. "Steady. . . . Pull. . . . Steady. . . . Pull. . . ." His hoarse voice boomed.

The crewmen braced themselves on the benches, half-closed their eyes, and rowed with all their might. The water poured down their necks and seeped through their linsey-woolsey jackets and inside their buckskin pantaloons. Mike bore down heavily on his tiller, pulling first one way and then the other, as the tumultuous waves piled upon his boat from all sides.

Suddenly Micky shouted shrilly: "Look out there! We've snarled our stem in the Devil's Cauldron. We're bein' pulled an' hauled round an' round like a mill wheel."

When the rain slackened so that he could see, Mike thrust the tiller over hard, and shouted, "All together, pull. . . . Pull. . . . Pull. . . ."

The men gave all they had, and kept their oars in perfect rhythm. Slowly they freed *Light Foot* from the treacherous whirlpool. Mike guided the boat into the lee of Baker's Island, five miles below Cave-in-Rock.

"We may as well tie up here," said Mike. "We've had about enough for one day."

While the crewmen held *Light Foot* from drifting, Micky dragged the bowline ashore and fastened it to a cottonwood tree. He clambered over the rail, shook himself like a half-drowned dog, and sputtered, "Right now I feel like a mud turtle looking for mud."

"At least," cackled the Mocker, "you're no wetter than the rest of us."

Mike followed his men to the cabin. He threw off his sopping clothes, shook the water out of his hair and beard, and said with mock seriousness, "We're here, my merry men, not because we planned to be here, nor because we wanted to be here, but because the fickle ol' girl this time got the best of us."

"We can thank our lucky star," added the Mocker, "that she didn't decide to ram us down the middle o' that whirlpool."

Micky scowled. "Mocker, you can surely think o' the silliest things. Come on now, you old squawker, give us a merry tune."

The Mocker was equal to the occasion, and was ready with an improvised ballad.

> A soppin' wet mouse
> An' a soppin' wet cat
> Set out for a feast
> And that was that.
> Singing *Hey diddle, diddle,*
> Singing *Hey diddle, dee.*
>
> The mouse ate cheese
> An' the cat ate sprat,
> And both had a feast,
> And that was that.
> Singing *Hey diddle, diddle,*
> Singing *Hey diddle, dee.*
>
> But the cat was greedy,
> And the cat ate the mouse;
> And the cat had a feast,
> And that was that.
> Singing *Hey diddle, diddle,*
> Singing *Hey diddle, dee.*

"Thank you, Mocker," said Mike grinning. "And now, Micky, stir your bones, an' set us up some victuals. We're all hungry enough to gnaw chunks off the hatch an' bunks."

"You're right, Cap'n Mike," said the Mocker. "Bestir yourself, Micky, before I start chewin' on my fiddle."

The rain began to pour again, and the keelboat tugged and
swayed at its mooring. Micky couldn't get outside to start a fire.
He opened a bag of Indian pemmican he kept on hand for just
such occasions, and uncorked a jug of apple cider. The men fell
to with a will, and then lay down in their bunks to relax.

Mike had sensed danger the moment he was forced to tie up
so near Cave-in-Rock, but said nothing to his men. They had
worked hard, and he was glad to let them sleep, if they wished.
However, he primed his horse pistol, and saw that his war club
was handy. He stretched out near the hatch, and kept himself
awake by thinking over the many exciting fights he had won
from one end of the river to the other. Near the middle of the
night he thought he heard a faint lapping of oars.

Lifting the hatch quietly, he peered into the darkness outside.
As he listened, the sounds grew more distinct. Two boats were
approaching from the direction of Cave-in-Rock.

Mike closed the hatch, and lighted a candle. He shook each
man, and said to him in an undertone: "Awake! Awake and out!
We're about to be boarded by the villains from Cave-in-Rock."

The men rolled out of their bunks, slipped on their buckskin
pantaloons, primed their horse pistols, and grabbed up their war
clubs. They scurried out on deck without saying a word. The
rhythmic dip of the approaching oars grew louder and louder.

"Bring on the bloody robbers," whispered Micky in a whirlwind of suppressed excitement.

The boats were now so near that Mike and his men could
hear the hoarse whisper of the robbers. "Board 'em, an' blow
'em down. . . . Ransack their craft, an' throw every last man

in the river to drown." The replies came fast and clear. "Ay, sir." "That we will, sir." "Yes, and with a right good will."

Mike's horse pistol spit fire, and there came a piercing cry from the boat. Mike's men fired their pistols and brandished their war clubs.

From the darkness came return pistol fire. A minute later a dozen daredevils clambered over the cargo box. Mike's men brought them down with their war clubs. There was wild yelling and shrieking, and the crash of bare fists. As fast as Mike and his men sent one attacker back into the river, two more came to take his place. Soon the *Light Foot* was crowded with robbers and crewmen in bitter combat.

In the darkness it was hard for the crewmen to tell their own men from the robbers. When the fight seemed to be about over, Mike brought a candle from the cabin, and found the Mocker on his back, at the mercy of Creole Charley. "You fool Frenchie," boomed Mike, laying a firm hand on Charley's shoulder, "can't you see it's Mocker you're chokin' to death? Lay off him, you idiot."

As soon as the decks were cleared, Mike and his men returned to the cabin. Mike had a bullet wound in his scalp. Micky's left eye was swollen shut, and blood trickled from his right shoulder. The Mocker's throat was so nearly swollen shut that he gasped for breath. There was not a man but had scratches and bruises, but neither was there one who was not proud of his part in the fight.

The men had returned to their bunks when Mike felt the bowlines part and knew that *Light Foot* had been set adrift. "The villains have cut our moorings," boomed Mike, lifting the hatch. "To the galley, my merry men!"

Mike sprang to the sweep and his crewmen to their oars. Through the foaming freshet they navigated *Light Foot* till dawn. As soon as Mike could get his bearings, he shouted: "We're now alongside Walker's Bar, an' lucky to be afloat. Steady on your oars while we move in behind this island. We're all in need of rest an' refreshment. We'll tie up here till this flash flood passes."

Soon *Light Foot* was riding proudly at-anchor. The morning sun came bright and warm, and Micky served breakfast on deck.

"What a night!" said the Mocker in a hoarse whisper.

Micky laughed, and put his hand up to his swollen eye. "Bless me, it's been just the kind o' child's play I most enjoy. What you say, Captain Mike — let's lay over here till nightfall, an' then row forward an' anchor below Cave-in-Rock again? Under cover of darkness we'll go ashore, an' once and for all put an end to them robbers an' murderers."

The Mocker had trouble clearing his throat. "Better put it off till next voyage."

"I'm sorry I choked you," said Creole Charley, nursing a long gash across his forehead. "I thought I was fightin' the robber that clubbed me."

Micky grinned maliciously. "I see we'll have to leave you on board, Mocker, when we make the attack tonight. You're no good at fightin' nohow."

"Leave me behind!" sniffed the Mocker hoarsely. "I'll say you don't!"

"You two varmints quit your sparrin'," said Mike, grinning. "It's high time we laid plans for the attack. Speak up, all of you, an' tell me what you think. I'm listenin'."

Each man told how he thought the assault should be made.

Mike spoke up, finally. "Each o' you has poured in his pail o' maple sap. Now, tell me what you think o' the sirup I've brewed. . . . We'll follow Micky's advice an' wait here at anchor till nightfall. We'll navigate *Light Foot* into the lee of Cave-in-Rock, as Mocker suggests, an' land our yawl on the creek below the robbers' hideout. Under cover of night, we'll advance silent as a herd o' deer, an' take the robbers by surprise."

"An' what a surprise she'll be!" said Micky, as excited as a monkey. "Each of us, exceptin' Mocker, 'll get his man. An' you, Captain Mike, you'll bowl down all the rest o' the gang!"

"There you go again, confound you," said the Mocker. "I promise to get as many of them as you, Micky."

"While we're relaxin', Mocker," said Mike, his eyes twinkling, "we could use one o' your merry tunes to help pass the time. It's too bad you're out o' voice."

"My voice may be ragged, but I can still manage to squeak."

> Oh, the sailor's life is a jolly, jolly life —
> Sing, ye merry men, sing;
> Oh, the sailor's life is a very jolly life —
> We fight an' we work through the jolly, jolly day,
> An' we fight an' we dance all the jolly, jolly night,
> An' our oars we man all the mornin'.
> Oh, the sailor's life is a jolly, jolly life —
> We work an' we fight an' we dance an' we sing —
> Sing, ye merry men, sing,
> Yes, sing, ye merry men, sing.

Striking up a different melody, the Mocker called hoarsely, "Come here, Creole Charley. Come dance a jig to this tune. If you're still as lively as you was when you was afightin' me last night, you'll sure give us a jolly, jolly jig."

Creole Charley came forward, smiling broadly at the Mocker's good humor. Forgetting his bruises and pains, he danced a lively turn.

Thus in song and dance they passed the rest of the day.

When twilight fell, Mike spoke to his men in a low, calm voice. "My merry men, I've a mighty lively little party planned for you tonight. We may as well come to grips with the Cave-in-Rock bandits now as any time."

The men were all ready to shout at once, but Mike silenced them. "We got to be as quiet and sly as foxes. Get your weapons in hand. Once we've made a landing, there's no time to lose."

The Mocker smiled. "We'll surprise even you this time, Captain."

"There's nothing new about that," said Micky, grinning. "You're always fuller of the wrong kind of surprises than a dog with fleas."

"Now that night has set in, it's time to make the start," said Mike as he firmly grasped the prow of the yawl. "Steady, there. Let her down easy without making any splash. That's fine. Now man your oars, my merry men."

Mike took his place in the stern. His war club was at his side. His horse pistol and long knife dangled from his belt. He cocked and primed Bang All, and cradled her across his left arm. No one even whispered. The oars moved in and out of the water with scarcely a ripple. The yawl moved forward as silent as a shadow.

They landed on a sandy beach, and dragged the yawl between clumps of willows. At Mike's heels the men moved forward. When they were within earshot of the Cave, they halted and listened and explored with their eyes. The lazy lapping of the water, the call of a hoot owl, and the cry of a lonesome whippoorwill were the only sounds. Then they saw the shadow of a lone sentry. Presently they heard voices that seemed to come from beyond the cave entrance.

"Let me go forward alone," Micky whispered in Mike's ear. "I'll see he doesn't sound a general alarm. Then you can come ahead without being discovered."

"Take it easy," whispered Mike. "Make yourself a ghost's shadow."

They watched as Micky crouched low, and started out on fox feet through the moonlight. Closer and closer he inched his way. A screech owl moaned woefully and a wolf from across the river howled. The hum of voices from beyond the cave rose to coarse laughter.

Micky threw himself upon the sentry. There was a dull thud as he hit the ground. Mike and his men crouched low and ran forward. They heard a boisterous shout, a general calling of names, and then the beginning of a free-for-all fight in a cabin a few paces beyond the cave entrance.

"This sentry here's but a striplin' lad," whispered Micky.

Mike looked at him. "Hope you've not done him bodily harm. . . . This is a lucky break for us. The outlaws are most likely gamblin' an' drinking. The cave seems deserted. Quick! Surround the cabin! When you are in your places I'll spring the bear trap. Get every man who tries to escape."

The men stationed themselves outside the doors and windows

of the cabin, their horse pistols drawn and their clubs ready. Mike leaped through the door, swinging his war club and fist. The gangsters were heavy with drink, and when they saw men being mowed down, they thought Mike a demon hot from hell. They bolted through the doors and windows so fast that many of them escaped and ran for cover like frightened bears. A number of bullets whizzed after them, but Micky and the others never knew if they took effect.

When the battle was won, Mike and his men filled their pockets with money scattered about the gaming tables and the floor. They dragged the stricken gamblers outside, fired the cabin and, in the lurid light, hurried back to their yawl.

On the way Mike paused a moment to examine the bruised sentinel, still lying where Micky had struck him down. "Why, strike me stone blind if this lad isn't a boy." Lifting the boy in his arms, he added, "I'll just tote you back to *Light Foot*, an' nurse your wounds." The feel of the lad's soft warm body awakened in Mike a strong fatherly emotion. Mike was too surprised and too happy to try to explain what was happening to him.

When they were at last safely aboard their craft, Micky was grinning from ear to ear. "We sure done a good job on that pack o' wolves."

"Yes, an' I helped," said the Mocker, his eyes twinkling.

"Thank you one an' all," said Mike, stepping astride the tiller. "They had it comin' to them, an' we give it to them hot an' heavy. . . . But you know what I'm thinkin'? The villains still have guns. We'd best get out o' here, and fast. So man your oars, my merry men. It's still a long way to New Orleans."

LEF

9.   A Mascot and an Earthquake

When morning came *Light Foot* was well on her way. Whenever Mike could find a minute to spare, he was at the young sentinel's side, nursing his wounds, and making him feel at home. The boy said his name was Carpenter. He also said he was happy to escape from the outlaws at Cave-in-Rock.

"We'll just make you our mascot," said Micky, as he set about preparing food. "That's just what we'll do."

The Mocker stopped fiddling long enough to add, "Yes, an' you better bring us a lot o' good luck, if you know what's good for you."

"Don't you worry, lad," said Mike. "Micky, you fetch Carpenter a slice o' that venison steak."

After they had eaten their meal, Mike turned to Carpenter and said, "Look here, son, when I was a boy your age I liked nothing better than to shoot mark. Now take hold o' Bang All."

He gave his faithful gun a loving caress as he handed it to the boy. "See how close you can come to knockin' the eye out o' that crow perched on yonder cottonwood."

The crewmen looked at each other in surprise. This was the first time Mike had ever allowed anyone to touch his precious rifle. If anyone suggested he'd like to try a practice shot, Mike always said, "Keep hands off. I've had a hard time trainin' Bang All to hit the nail on the head. I can't take any chance o' having her learn wild habits."

Young Carpenter took up the gun, examined it carefully, and then stared wide-eyed at the crow. He squinted through the sights, and the muzzle quivered as if it had the ague. He pointed Bang All in the general direction of the crow, blinked his eye and pulled the trigger. For a long minute the crow didn't even move, and then it simply curved its neck, and gave three saucy caws.

"You see, Mr. Fink," said Carpenter innocently, "this is the first time I've tried shooting."

Micky had all he could do to keep from exploding in laughter. "Sakes alive, my boy, his name's *Captain* Mike."

Mike smiled kindly. "Don't you worry none about missin' that fool crow, son. As soon as we reach Natchez, I'm goin' to buy you the finest long rifle that ever was made. You're goin' to practice every day till you can bark a squirrel or shoot the eye out of a flying swan."

"I can't promise you much," said Carpenter doubtfully.

"Considering this was your first shot from a movin' boat, you done mighty well." Mike added, keeping his eye peeled for sawyers and floating islands: "Why, when I was a boy your age, I was so dumb I didn't know which end of a rifle you were supposed to hold to your shoulder. I figured mebbe you laid the bullet in the middle of the pan, an' fired the gun by holding a lighted candle to the powder. Then it was Uncle Charley took me in hand, and showed me what a firearm was used for. I figure it don't hurt any lad to have an old head teach him tricks."

Micky had to have his joke. "Captain Mike, I'll bet you two to one the lad can hit the side o' *Light Foot*'s cabin — that is, if you put him inside and close the hatch."

"Don't you mind him none, son. In a week or two you'll be shootin' straighter than Micky ever shot."

The Mocker laid his fiddle across his knees. "Say, boy, you see that swamp hole side o' that creek mouth there? I happen to know there's plenty o' quicksand under that peaceful muck. I never pass this place without rememberin' what happened here the first time I sailed down this river years ago. My partner an' me come driftin' by in a dugout canoe. I saw a wide-brimmed beaver hat floatin' on the surface, kind o' twitchin', but not much. I reached out my long paddle an' tried to fish the hat into the boat. An' you know what?" Mocker looked up and grinned. "Believe it or not, a man's head bobbed up out o' that muck, an' said, after blowin' the mud an' water out o' his mouth, 'Stranger, keep hands off. Don't try to rob me of my only hat.' 'But don't you need some kind o' help?' I asked, a little astonished. 'Leave me alone!' said the stranger, disgusted. 'If you think this is the first sinkhole I been in durin' my migration West to the Plains, you're badly mistaken. What's the matter with your eyes?' An' then I nearly jumped out o' the canoe in surprise. The stranger yanked on his reins, an' up come the head of a horse, ablowin' an' asnortin' mud an' water all over the place!"

Carpenter opened his eyes so wide and looked so astonished

that the crewmen chuckled louder at him than at Mocker's "fool
yarn."

By the time they had quieted down, the Mocker was fiddling
and chanting.

> A young lad went asailin',
> Asailin' on the river;
> The captain manned the tiller
> An' what it took he give 'er.
> They sweat an' pushed an' bushwhacked;
> They fought through sun and rain;
> They kept her movin' forward
> Over the boundin' main.
> They sailed without a sorrow;
> They sailed without a fear;
> On many a merrie voyage
> They sailed for many a year.

Micky shrugged his shoulders. "It's about my turn to spin a
yarn. And, lad, this story o' mine's a true story. And this actually happened right here around Hull's Point, at that creek
mouth you see yonder. Cap'n Billy was navigatin' our craft, an'
this was years ago, when we were sailin' downstream. Suddenly
two white men, their shirts an' pants in shreds, started runnin'
along the shore, wavin' their arms an' giving piteous cries for
help. 'We're lost, an' we're starvin' to death!' they moaned.
'Take us on board! Save us! Save us!'

"All this struck us so quick we didn't have time to think
things over. Captain Billy threw his sweep around hard, an' the
Half Moon (that was the original name o' this boat, Carpenter) swung around toward the creek mouth. What would have
happened next, no one can say for certain, if Cap'n Billy hadn't

happened to spy an Injun nose stickin' between the wild cane stocks. Quicker'n you can say 'Scat!' he swung his sweep round tother way, an' shouted, 'Put all you got into your oars, men! Row! Row! Row!'

"But old chickenhearted Mocker didn't even then sense the danger, an' begged Cap'n Billy to turn back. By that time the Injuns was swarmin' on shore thicker'n blackberries, apepperin' us with their feathered arrows. Cap'n Billy had his shirt most torn off him, an' then an arrow carried his cap a hundred feet an' more out in the river. We sure burned a channel down the river, with Cap'n Billy steerin' a zigzag course to escape most o' the arrows."

"Only thing that saved us," drawled the Mocker, "was Micky's bein' so bad scared. He rowed so fast an' furious no Injun canoe could ever hope to keep in arrow shot o' us."

"Don't believe a word of it, lad," barked Micky. "Old Mocker, for once in his indolent life, was so scared he rowed as hard as the rest o' us."

"But we didn't blame the white captives," said Captain Mike for Carpenter's benefit. "The treacherous Indians forced them to cry for help, in the hope of waylaying us."

The Mocker began fiddling a jig, and when he had finished it, he said to Carpenter, "You should'ave been with us the day Micky got smart an' started pickin' on a Pennsylvania Dutchman. It happened upstream where you see that eagle's nest in the top of that towerin' poplar. The Dutchman was navigatin' his driftin' flat, an' mindin' his own business. As *Light Foot* was passin' near him, Micky reached out with his long oar an' gave the stranger a love pat over the head, hard enough to crown a mule. The Dutchman keeled over, an' when he come to, he looked hard at Micky. 'Vat for you crack my head?' he shouted. Micky told him, 'A mosquito hit you, that's what it was.'

"Then quicker'n you can bat an eye, that Dutchman grabbed up a fistful o' walnuts he'd gathered along the way, an' began peltin' Micky like a hailstorm. By the time that Dutchman finally run out o' ammunition, Micky had a dozen bumps on his head an' shoulders — bigger'n hen's eggs. An' you should'ave seen Micky's eyes! They were stickin' out like glossy buckeyes, so big you could knock 'em off with a war club. The Dutchman danced in glee and shouted, 'Dat'll teach ye, ye snarlin' wolf pup, not to stick yer head in de mouth o' the next b'ar ye meet!'

"But you can't learn an old dog new tricks. Micky's been just as bad as he was before. A porcupine's a porcupine, always throwin' his pizen quills at you."

Micky sniffed and snarled. "That's a silly yarn, Carpenter. Let me tell you another true story. This happened one day after we'd safely run the Falls. We were needing some meat for dinner an' I argued half an hour tryin' to get Mocker to lay down his useless fiddle long enough to catch us a mess o' catfish. Finally, he said if I'd bait his hook for him an' take off any fish he happened to catch, he'd see what he could do. When I was in the middle of makin' the meal, Mocker yelled he thought he'd snagged bottom. 'Hold on, you sucker!' I shouted. 'Don't you dare throw that line overboard. If you're too lazy to pull 'er in, wrap the line around the sweep lock.' Sure enough, the lazy Mocker fastened his line, and went back to his monotonous fiddlin'. When I could spare a minute from the victuals, I hurried over to see what Lazybones had hooked. 'Come on back here, you lazy tadpole, and land your catch!' I shouted. 'If I never hear you play that gratin' fiddle again, 'twill be too soon!'

"After he'd sawed another discordant tune, I finally got him back on his job. He pulled till he had blisters on every one o' his ladylike fingers. When at last he saw the fish's big mouth, Mocker let out a yell to raise the dead, an' run back to the middle o' the boat. I saw it was an enormous yellow channel catfish, an' grabbed up the slack line. I landed next thing to a whale. That catfish weighed sixty pounds. But poor white-livered Mocker didn't enjoy the savory steaks I served from his fish. Every time he looked at one, he shivered for fear the fish would bite him!"

The Mocker cackled in glee: "Now let me tell a true, true one. One day we ran into a fog so thick it made a perfect fool o' Micky. Micky was so badly fooled he made up his pallet on the fog out over the gunnel! Why, that fog was so thick you couldn't see nothin'. Well, all went well till Micky rolled out on the pallet to sleep. He broke through the crust on that fog, an' we had to turn to and fish the half-drowned tadpole out o' the river. . . ."

Micky and the Mocker couldn't be blamed too much for capping each other's tall yarns. As the tales grew taller and taller, Carpenter's eyes opened wider and wider. Mike and his men were kept busy entertaining their mascot.

This happy mood continued for several days. Then — to be exact, at about two o'clock on a bright moonlight morning — there was a violent change. *Light Foot* was riding at anchor in the lee of Diamond Island, and the men were in their bunks asleep. Mike was awakened when the boat began dancing and pitching. There came a sullen rumbling that ended in a heavy cannonlike crash.

Mike rolled out of bed. "We're boarded by outlaws!" he

shouted. "Grab your horse pistols and war clubs. To the deck!"

As Mike lifted the hatch, *Light Foot* gave a violent lurch that sent him tumbling smack against the cargo box. On shore there was a terrific din and turmoil. Trees crashed, rocks creaked and crumbled as the earth buckled and lurched.

A minute later the crewmen came staggering to the tossing deck.

"What in all tarnation?" growled Micky, half awake. "What is this? Must be one o' Mocker's nightmarish tales. Let's get back to our bunks!"

At this moment there came another terrifying rumble ending in a sharp thunderous explosion. The river shook itself like an aroused alligator, trees crashed, and the shores crumbled and flowed like cold molasses into the boiling water.

"A tall tale, indeed!" the Mocker jeered, clutching the side of the dancing cargo box. "Anybody with half an eye can see the world's comin' to a sudden bad end!"

The next shock parted the bowlines. "Man the oars!" boomed Mike. "Row for your lives! We're bein' swamped under this crumblin' riverbank, an' about to be overwhelmed by falling trees!"

Despite the wild lurching of *Light Foot*, the men executed the command and Mike navigated to the center of the current.

Again there came a deep ominous rumble and another sharp report like the crack of doom. The shores shook themselves violently, tossing the trees about like a child's playthings, and dashing the shattered earth into the boiling river. Springs gushed up from the river bottom on all sides of *Light Foot* like spouting whales. The hapless boat was driven first in one direction and then in another. Constantly the current changed direction. Mike and his men gave their last ounce of strength to navigate *Light Foot*, so that her prow cut the seething waves square across. Suddenly Mike saw a great tidal wave rise above the tumult and advance upstream.

By a miracle of brute strength he spun *Light Foot* around to meet the wall of water. *Light Foot*'s prow lifted like a rearing stallion and then plunged forward. The men were nearly carried from the galley by the onrushing water.

The confused noises of the earth tremor died down, and the men became aware of screaming wild ducks and geese and swans. Water birds of all kinds flew squawking in terror. On the shore, owls screeched shrilly and eagles screamed. Deer bugled as they ran, bears snuffed and wolves howled dismally.

For the first time in his life Micky was really scared. He threw his arms above his head and wailed, "This *is* the Day of Doom!"

"First it's nightmares, an' now the Day of Doom," boomed Mike. "Can't you see, you fool Thunderbolt? This is the biggest earthquake of all time! An' here we are with ringside seats, in the very middle of it! Now quit your fussin' an' pull steady on the oars. *Light Foot*'s not beaten in this fight; no, not by a long shot!"

A few minutes later the upstream tidal wave spent itself, and the backwater it had carried with it broke through. It sent *Light Foot* dashing downstream on the crest of the current so fast the hard-bitten crewmen crouched low and held their breath. When *Light Foot* scraped and bounded over a riffle, Micky again was scared. "This is the Day o' Doom, sure enough! A blind man could see that!"

Thanks to Mike's navigation and the strange chances of For-

tune, *Light Foot* rode out the thousand perils of that terrific night. When daylight came they found the boat floating amidst innumerable hazards. Trees and bushes on all sides were riding abreast the angry muddy waters. Many newly formed sawyers and wooden islands were planted in unknown places. Tops of drifting trees scraped their keel, and hidden snags lay in wait to split them wide open.

"Keep your oars tossed, my merry men," shouted Mike. "We'll slip in behind Hurricane Island, an' tie up till the commotion is over."

With powerful muscle and unflagging will they brought *Light Foot* to anchor, the dashing current swirling by on either side.

Suddenly Mike thought of Carpenter. "Where's the boy?" he shouted, and without waiting a reply, dashed down to the cabin. The men listened breathlessly. "Why, here you are!" they heard Mike exclaim. "Are you all right?"

Carpenter awoke, and wondered why Mike was shaking him. "Yes, Captain Mike — why, what's happened?"

Mike slapped his thigh, and roared in laughter. "What's happened! Why, my lad, you've slept through the biggest show on earth. We've had a terrible earthquake!"

"An earthquake!" Carpenter gasped, rolling out of bed, and pulling on his clothes. "Why didn't you tell me sooner?"

Again Mike slapped his thigh. "Why, we were too busy keepin' *Light Foot* afloat. If we were all as sleepy-headed as you, we'd now be on the bottom of the river."

After the men had finished their breakfast the Mocker picked up his fiddle and began playing. Suddenly he pulled his fiddle down from his chin and laid it across his knees, and burst out laughing. "So you was sure, my darlin' Micky, you was crossin' the River Styx. You was that scared your eyes was poppin' out o' their shells like buckeyes."

"You was as scared as anybody, an' you know it," growled Micky. "It was you that first thought it was the Day o' Doom!"

Later in the day there came another ominous rumbling and another crash. This, however, was not nearly as severe as the others. *Light Foot* danced and lunged at her tether, but luckily the bowlines held. This time it was Carpenter who was scared. He clung to the side of the cargo box, afraid of being thrown overboard.

"Don't you worry, son," said Mike, smiling. "Danger is as scared of us as you are of it."

A week later *Light Foot* sailed out into the mighty Mississippi, and left behind the last traces of the devastating earthquake. But no one could forget the tremendous experience. Mocker made up a song about it:

> Old Mother Earth grew weary
> O' laying in her bunk,
> Old Mother Earth got weary, weary,
>
> O' laying in her bunk
> For a thousand years an' more, an' more,
> For a thousand years an' more.
>
> So suddenly she shook her,
> So up she got an' shook her,
> She danced in mad an' wicked glee.
>
> Then down she lay to rest her,
> We hope for a thousand years an' more,
> For a thousand years an' more.

While the Mocker was chanting and Micky was snarling at him, Mike turned the tiller over to Carpenter. "Son, you got not only to know how to shoot a rifle, but beginnin' right now you'll get lessons from me on how to use this tiller."

"Very well, Captain Mike," said Carpenter obediently. His sharp features grew tense as he focused his attention on his new job. The afternoon sun was warm, and the breeze balmy. The current ran straight as a ramrod. Mike stretched out on the cargo box to relax, but he still kept a sharp lookout ahead.

The crewmen pretended not to notice what was happening, but they were alert, ready to spring into action at the first call in any emergency.

10. "Witch" Craft

Mike was now in his prime and he thought nothing of the passing of a year or two. Astride his tiller, he was a handsome, powerful, dominating figure. His glossy black beard was as thick as bear fur, and he had the shaggy mane of a stallion. He was clad in red shirt, fringed blue surtout that reached almost to his knees, buckskin pantaloons, and Indian moccasins. His red woolen sash and jaunty coonskin cap were the finishing touches for a fine figure of a man.

Mike was king of all he surveyed. He was the toast of every tavern along the river. Men raised their glasses "To the Snapping Turtle of the O-hi-o-o and the Snag of the Massassip!" In his cap he flaunted a jaunty red feather, the insignia of his undisputed prowess.

No one rose to challenge Mike when he said playfully, "I've growed a porcupine quill for every mosquito bite I suffered when a young boatman. Yes, an' if all the cock-a-doodles I've subdued was laid end to end, they'd reach all the way from Pittsburgh to New Orleans. Anybody 'round here want me to show 'em how the trick's done?"

In every tavern, men talked of the moving frontier. "Why, even I can remember when Pittsburgh was just a fort in the fork o' the rivers," said Mike to Captain Keefer of the *Crescent Star*, in the tavern at Limestone. "Now see what a city she is. She makes almost everything, an' there's nothin' she don't make you can't buy in her stores."

"Yes, and the same thing's true of Louisville," said Keefer, smacking his lips. "Why, only a few years ago, when I first started navigatin', she was just one lone house on a high hill. And now she's puttin' on airs like a struttin' turkey cock, an' braggin she's the biggest and best city west o' Pittsburgh."

"Only trouble is," added Mike, "I'm havin' a harder and harder time shootin' a deer or a turkey from the boat, the way I used to do. Now all I ever see is homesteaders cuttin' down the forests. It's a nuisance having so many villages springin' up everywhere."

"That may be true, Mike, but don't forget the more folks there are, the more goods we have to carry. An' if it wasn't for the homesteaders, our keelboats would have to battle their way upstream without any cargo."

"You're right. We shouldn't worry about anything."

"At least *you* shouldn't, Mike. Everybody knows your *Light Foot*'s the fastest an' safest keelboat afloat. Yes, an' you carry the hardiest crew, an' the best disciplined, an' the best paid. An' what's more, you're always able to pick up the most valuable cargo that pays the highest freight rate."

The tavern keeper, Henry Harper, listened to every word. He cleared his throat. "Only thing worryin' me is the wagon roads. I hear they're bein' used by more an' more families. An' besides, they tell me there is a new invention they call a steamboat somewhere back East in the tideland."

Mike roared in laughter. "Don't you lose any sleep, Henry. Only thing worryin' me is that there are too many boats on the river. Why, they're multiplyin' faster'n mosquitoes in wet May weather."

Mike was so busy with his own work that he did not have time to think of what was happening in the rest of the world. He didn't know that the rapid expansion of the frontier had set men's minds aflame. Inventors were working on machines suited for the needs of the New World. Oliver Evans and James Watt had dreamed up a freight wagon that would run on a firm wooden track, and be pulled by a steam engine; their dream was being realized in the first railroad. John Fitch had been working night and day to find some way to attach a steam engine to a boat, and, after years of heartbreak and failure, his dream was blossoming out into the first steamboat.

But Mike and his race of alligator-horse men saw nothing to fear. Their wills and their muscles were tireless as spring steel. They bragged they had the toughest, hardest job in the world. They dragged and pushed their keelboats against the merciless current, and dared the fickle old girl to do her worst.

"Why, I wouldn't think o' tradin' jobs with anybody,"

boomed Mike, his eyes shining. "Compared with keelboatin', everything else is petticoat work."

This way things went on for another year. Then, one day while the Mocker was seated amidships facing Mike and sawing away at his fiddle, he saw a most unusual craft astern. He continued to stare at the specter as it rapidly approached, and finally called Mike's attention to the strange boat.

"She's most likely some new keelboat on her maiden voyage," said Mike after a cursory glance. "She's just tryin' to show off. We'll take it easy till she comes alongside, and then we'll show her greenhorn captain our tail feathers!"

"She seems uncommon high in the deck," observed Micky after a few minutes. "An' if my eyes don't deceive me, she's wallowing in foam. Must be she's one o' Mocker's mythical sea serpents."

"You sure do have a crazy imagination," said Mike, without even taking a second glance.

"There's somethin' mighty strange about the craft," insisted Micky. "She's a-bearin' down on our tail like a young tornado. Bless my soul, for the first time in his life ol' Mocker's right. She does have a sea of white water on both sides o' her."

Mike turned and stared so long that *Light Foot* began to veer from the center of the current. "What in the nation can she be?" he asked. "I'll bet she's some 'witch' craft!"

"Well, knock my eyes off with a shillalah!" said Micky, excited. "I never thought I'd live to see a whale of a keelboat like this! Why, she's four times as long, an' twice as high, an' three times faster than *Light Foot!*"

"Hold your tongue," snarled Mike, losing his temper. "*Light*

Foot is the best boat on the river, you know that. Yes, an' she's the best boat there ever will be!"

As the strange craft drew nearer, the men saw a span of bay horses in the center of the upper deck being driven in a circle around a vertical shaft. By a series of concealed wooden gears this shaft was attached to a horizontal water wheel at either side of the boat. These side wheels were spinning around in a sea of foam, and the boat was racing downstream at what seemed an incredible speed to Mike and his men.

Mike stood tense as steel at his tiller, his face purple with rage. Then he stamped his right foot with a resounding crash, and boomed: "Man the oars! We'll show these Yankees they can't trick us like this! *Pull. . . . Pull. . . . Pull. . . . Pull-l-l.*"

In his anger and excitement Mike called a cadence so fast that no oarsman could follow it with long heavy keelboat oars. When the boat came within earshot, Mike boomed angrily, "What kind o' Yankee trick you tryin' to play on us!"

"Dis is de *Flying Dutchman*," shouted the proud German captain. "Dis is fastest boat ever to sail dis Inland Vatervay!"

"You're a lot o' cutthroats, that's what you are!" shrieked Mike, quite out of temper. "You're robbers, stealing honest traffic from honest rivermen, propelling your craft with horses!"

"You know de trouble mitt you?" answered the captain, smiling. "You got de strong back an' arm, but de weak mind. Dese horses eat only hay an' drink river vater. Your alligator-horses, dey eat meat, flour, drink peach brandy. All expensive victuals!"

"If ever I lay hands on you," yelled Mike as the *Flying Dutchman* plowed ahead, "I'll drive you off this river if I have to lick the moccasins off you an' throw you in the ragin' torrent to drown!"

"Ven do de tadpole expect to ketch de flyin' swan?"

"For twopence I'd let the daylight into you with Bang All!"

"In dis cockfight you been licked before you start. Ve got de brains, you got only de expensive labor!"

By this time the *Flying Dutchman* was so far in the lead that even Mike's booming voice was lost on the wind.

This was the first defeat Mike had ever suffered since he started sailing. He stood astride his tiller, his feet planted like rock, his chin up. For a long time he said nothing. His men knew enough to keep silent, too. Finally Mike moved the tiller and brought *Light Foot* back into the center of the current. A smile played around his eyes.

"The fickle ol' girl'll soon show that smart captain where to head in. His crazy *Flyin' Dutchman*'s too all-fired fast to survive the treachery of these waterways!"

"We all know you're right," said Micky, loyal to his master.

"Of course I'm right!" snapped Mike. "You just wait till she flies into Horsetail Ripple, or comes suddenly up against Letart's Falls, or tries to slip past the Devil's Elbow! Why, she'll be ripped wide open from stem to stern. We're bound to find wreckage, timbers an' cargo an' all, scattered over the sands an' shoals, long before we end this voyage."

"Looks bad to me," sighed the Mocker, fiddling a sad tune.

"Trouble with you," snarled Mike, "is you're always havin' bad dreams. If you had a grain o' sense you'd know there's no better boat afloat anywhere than *Light Foot!*"

"You're right, Captain," added Micky. "Mocker's never been right about anything but once. An' he'll never be right again."

The Mocker fiddled away, without saying anything.

"We're not beat yet," continued Mike. "No sir-ee, not by a

long shot! We'll overtake that bird o' passage an' pluck out all her tail feathers long before we reach New Orleans!"

"I'll bet you two to one, Mocker," bantered Micky, "that Cap'n Mike is right."

"Hoist the sail, my merry men!" boomed Mike. "We got a tail wind."

The wind filled the sail, and *Light Foot*, airy and fleet, skipped down the current.

The days that followed were uneventful. Mike seemed restless. His eyes were always glued on the water ahead, scanning every inch of the channel. "It'll be nothin' short of a miracle," he repeated a hundred different times, "if that *Flyin' Dutchman* ever reaches New Orleans."

Two weeks went by, and then one day *Light Foot* met the *Sky Rocket* laboring upstream. Mike called out to Captain Lowry: "Seen anything of a 'witch' craft called the *Flying Dutchman?*"

"Sure I seen her," answered Lowry, excited. "She tied up at Natchez the morning we left. That's now a week ago day before yeste'day. Been lookin' for her to pass me now for three days. Believe me, she's the latest marvel for speed. She's hung up such a fast record down from Pittsburgh that there's no other boat good enough to be considered even a second to her. Even your *Light Foot*'s never come within three weeks of equalin' what this marvel's just done."

For the moment not only Mike but also his men were stunned and speechless. Their world was crumbling beneath them as in a tremendous earthquake.

"This *Flying Dutchman*," continued Lowry, growing more

and more excited, "sure makes one wonder what's the use o' wastin' all this elbow grease on a keelboat, when two corn-and-oats horses can triple in speed the best we can hope to do. My eyes begin to see a vision o' churnin' side-wheelers fillin' this river, an' speedin' up traffic. I feel us keelboaters are sunk. Why, a fellow down at Natchez tells me that back in the Tidewater country they're rigging up steam engines hitched to side-wheelers. Makes me wonder, Captain Mike, if we've not had our day. Soon they'll be storing our keelboats along with Noah's Ark in some museum."

"But for all you say, Captain Lowry, I'm still bettin' you two to one the flirtin' ol' girl will lure that *Flying Dutchman* to destruction before she can be navigated back to Pittsburgh!"

As long as they were within earshot, Captain Lowry kept up his flow of prophecy. But Mike laughed it off with a simple shrug of his shoulders.

"Just you wait and see!" he yelled at the top of his register. "I'll cover any amount of money you want to put up. Yes, an' I'll still give you two to one!"

Three days later Mike navigated *Light Foot* around a sharp bend in the river, and came in full view of Horsetail Ripple. Quickly he scanned the waters. His face lighted up like a torch, and his grin spread from ear to ear.

He pointed with his stubby forefinger, and shouted, "What did I tell you! See, Mocker, there's your 'witch' craft, settled down tight on the snag that ripped her keel wide open. She's ridin' up to her deck in mud!"

"This is about the seven-hundredth time you been wrong, Mocker," roared Micky.

The Mocker just smiled. He began a merry tune, and fiddled away as if he had not heard what Micky said.

As Mike navigated *Light Foot* safely through the treacherous narrows, the men saw that the *Flying Dutchman* had been abandoned.

"They must have swum the horses ashore," said Mike. "But they've left their proud boat, an' most of its cargo, I'll bet you, to the flirtin' ol' girl."

Ten days later Mike tied up at New Orleans to dispose of his cargo. The merchants and boatsmen were very much excited over the magic record of the *Flying Dutchman*. Colonel Bisby greeted Mike at his warehouse door, and began talking excitedly.

"Well, Captain Mike, old boy, the day of wonders has just begun! Your proud record between Pittsburgh and this dock has been smashed to smithereens. The *Flying Dutchman* has not only beat your record, but she has clipped thirty-eight days an' four hours off the quickest voyage your *Light Foot* ever made. Believe it or not, this is a fact."

Mike waited in silence, and gave Colonel Bisby plenty of rope.

"Looks to me, Captain Mike," continued the colonel, his tongue wagging at both ends, "as if the days of the keelboat are numbered. Everybody these days is calling for speed and more speed. Somebody was sure to invent some new kind of craft to give the merchants and manufacturers what they have been demanding. The keelboat was never speedy, especially upstream, but it was the best boat we had. Yes, and we've made good use of it! But now, at long last, we have a new and faster kind of river navigation. This *Flying Dutchman* has turned the trick. She's shortened the downstream passage by nearly half. And if the claim of her captain proves true, she'll make the upstream voyage in one tenth the time it takes your lumbering *Light Foot*. Don't be mad with me for telling you all this. . . . Yes, and she has another advantage. She carries three times the cargo your *Light Foot* carries, and, what's more important, at one third the cost."

"That's what you think," said Mike, striking suddenly like a hidden snag. "There's one trouble with this newfangled crazy contraption — and that is, she's not safe. Why, even a fish can't swim upstream at the terrific speed o' that *Flyin' Dutchman* without scrapin' all its scales off against the sawyers, an' rippin' itself wide open on the snags an' rocks."

Colonel Bisby sniffed impatiently. "There's one trouble with you, too, Captain. You're living in the past age. Wake up and look into the future."

"Why, the truth is, Colonel," continued Mike, a smile playing around his eyes, "even now — while you're braggin' yourself hoarse about this 'witch' craft — this very minute, she's settlin' in the mud just this side o' Horsetail Ripple! She's been deserted by her crew. Right now they're stumblin' back home along the Natchez Trace, totin' on the backs of their horses what few trinkets they could salvage from her cargo."

"You d-don't mean it?" stammered Colonel Bisby. "And to think — why, I shipped aboard the *Flying Dutchman* the cargo I had been saving for *Light Foot* . . . ! This is the biggest loss I've suffered in years."

"Could be you'll someday get your eyeteeth cut, Colonel,"

added Mike — his chin up and his eyes glowing — "that is, by the time you're old as Methuselah. But at the rate you're learnin', you'll still be plenty dumb by the time you're a thousand years old."

"I should have remembered the old hornbook maxim my mother taught me," moaned the colonel: "BE NOT THE FIRST BY WHOM THE NEW ARE TRIED."

"I wonder, Colonel, have you got anything left to barter?"

"I'm almost cleaned out, to the last cricket. But I'll see if I can't scrape together something."

By the time they had finished trading, Colonel Bisby's spirits were beginning to rebound. "You'll live to see, Captain, that in the long run I'm not entirely wrong. Here's that old hornbook maxim in full:

"Be not the first by whom the new are tried,
Nor yet the last to lay the old aside."

"If it makes you feel any better, Colonel, keep right on repeatin' it. But as for me, I've already forgot every word of it."

"And if you're not more careful, Captain, you're going to be left high and dry yourself. The day is near at hand when somebody will be smart enough to perfect a boat that will race over the riffles of these Inland Waterways faster'n an Injun can run through fire. If the sawyers and snags and wooden islands get in the way, why, the Government at Washington will step in and free the rivers of them. You know yourself, Captain, that the world never stands still. She's like our old Massassip, she keeps amoving all the while. I still believe your *Light Foot* has had her day. The night will settle down on all keelboats sooner than any of us think."

Again Mike waited patiently till the colonel had finished.

"For all you say, I'm still layin' my hard money on *Light Foot*. Why is it folks are so flighty and nervous, anyhow? They all want to run when they can walk just as well. They got nothing of importance to do when they get there. Speed don't make this world a better place to live in, you know that. Already the homesteaders are crowdin' the deer and b'ar back twenty miles from the river. Their barkin' dogs an' clackin' hens destroy the sweet silence. It's just like Uncle Charley used to say, folks don't know what freedom is. It's gettin' so a man can't spread his elbows without hittin' some feller in the ribs. By the way us human critters is buzzin' round, you'd think us all a nest o' angered hornets. I like to recall the time when I took Bang All an' wandered off through the woods. In an hour or two I'd have my turkey or deer or b'ar. That was the best time I can remember. Make all the noise about speed you want. Trouble with you is, you're barkin' up the wrong tree. These are my sentiments, Colonel. Yes, an' you'll do well to save your next cargo for *Light Foot*. She may be a little slow, as you say, but it won't cost you anything to play safe."

"You know, Captain," said the colonel, as the men were pulling in *Light Foot*'s shore lines, "we'll both do well to remember both ends of that old hornbook maxim. Then when we see a dancing steamboat prance up and down this old river, stirring up a breast wave that will wash all the catfish ashore — then, say, I hope we'll both be in the position to enjoy that glorious day."

"If that terrible day ever comes, Colonel, I'll strike out for the backwoods, further West. I hear there's plenty o' wilderness left up the Missouri. . . . So long, Colonel. Be seein' you again soon, I hope."

As Mike navigated *Light Foot* upstream, he shook his head time and again, trying to free his mind of the colonel's old hornbook maxim. But the harder he tried, the faster the maxim went around in his mind, like a piece of driftwood caught in a whirlpool.

"What you shakin' your head so often about?" asked Micky.

Mike shrugged his shoulders and grinned. "Oh, that? Why I'm just tryin' to shake out some nonsense the colonel planted in my mind. The words don't mean nothin', but they almost drive me crazy."

11.   The Vastness of the Lordly River

Mike and his men began to feel encumbered by the many new kinds of river craft set afloat by frontier ingenuity. They should not be blamed too much for being annoyed, since the river had so long belonged to them and *Light Foot*.

Mike was curious and amused, however, by Peter Plimpton's floating gristmill. Peter had attached a water wheel between two flats. By anchoring his craft in the current, and by gearing his millstone to his water wheel, he succeeded in using the perpetual free water power. He had the additional advantage of being able to go to his customers instead of asking them to come to him. This pleased the homesteaders, and soon Peter found himself the most prosperous millwright of his day.

"You got to admit," argued Micky, "that this Yankee is a clever feller."

"The old world's amovin', she's arifflin' right along," chanted the Mocker.

"But I don't like it!" boomed Mike. "Crazy crafts like Peter's do nothin' but clutter up traffic. They got no business on the river."

"But Peter's got more business," drawled the Mocker, "than a proverbial feather merchant in a high wind."

Other Yankees had been quick to imitate Peter Plimpton's initiative. Allan More started a floating store, stocked with a supply of dry goods and ready-made clothes, boots and bonnets, hardware and crockery. He navigated his large canoe with the help of his two sturdy sons. When he docked his boat, he donned a long white apron, and proved himself a better merchant than he was a sailor.

Others devised floating tin shops and blacksmith shops. They were all busy as bees, carrying their wares to every settlement, and adding to the comfort of frontier life.

Each of these floating stores carried a tin whistle. As the boat approached a landing place, the captain blew a series of blasts that sent the echoes flying in every direction. Someone on shore was certain to hear the signal and spread the news of the arrival. The captain made it a rule to carry a heavy cargo of free gossip, news, and general information so that everyone with time on his hands would come down to the dock, whether or not he needed supplies or had anything to barter.

Mike, when he was a boy, had learned to imitate the language of all living creatures. He now found it fitted his mood to imitate the tin whistles of the various merchants. Without difficulty he quickly memorized the tone and the number of blasts each captain sounded. He simply placed his forefinger and his thumb on either side of his tongue, puckered his lips, and blew a shrill note.

When the expectant settlers came hurrying down to the boat landing, Mike would shout out the different staples that made up his cargo: "Monongahela flour, Pittsburgh iron pigs, Kentuck salt, and O-hi-o-o peach brandy. Unless you want to buy something with hard money, I'll not bother to barter with you today."

Of course he knew in advance that no one would care to buy anything he had aboard. His deception, however, caused much merriment among his crew.

Sammy Smithers at Willow Creek Landing was always angry when Mike succeeded in fooling him. Mike took particular pleasure in imitating a different boat whistle each time he passed.

"You old skinflint!" Sammy shouted as soon as he realized he was fooled. "I'll get even with you! Just you see if I don't!"

Mike boomed in joy, "How's the weather on your Kentuck shore? She's pretty cool here on the river compared to the way you sound."

"She'll be hotter here than she is today," flared Sammy in a rage — "that is, if ever you dare tie up at my landing!"

"Take 'er cool there, Sammy!" Mike added in glee. "You're liable to be a lot hotter in the next world than you are now in this one!"

"I'll have the constable on you!" shrieked Sammy in high fury. "Why, you're nothin' but a flea-bitten skinflint, that's what you are!"

By this time Mike and his men were exploding in laughter. The Mocker couldn't contain himself, and broke forth in spontaneous song.

The Constable is comin',
The Constable is comin',
The Constable is comin' right away.
Yes, Sammy's lost his temper sure today.
Sing *High*, sing *High did, diddle*,
Sing *High*, sing *High did, diddle*,
The Constable is comin'; sing *Hurray!*

As a parting shot, Mike shouted, "Say, Sammy, can't I take your order for a barrel o' Orleans molasses or some Java coffee for delivery on the return voyage?"

"Why, you scoundrel! I wouldn't buy twopence worth o' nothin' from the likes o' you," shrieked the irate Sammy as he stumbled back to his tavern. "I wouldn't, even if your *Light Foot* was the only boat afloat in the world!"

One afternoon a week later Mocker was seated in his accustomed place on the cargo box, facing Mike at the sweep. He sighted plumes of smoke no bigger than a man's hand, that seemed to rise out of the water and drift slowly toward the right.

"Strike me blind," said the Mocker, after watching the strange object a long time, "if the river behind us hasn't caught afire!"

Micky was making the meal, and didn't even take time to look up. "Only trouble with you, Mocker, is you've had too long a cat nap."

"You ol' doubtin' Thomas," said the Mocker. "Try your own peepers, an' see what you can make out of it."

Micky strained his eyes. "Say, what do you know! I shouldn't wonder if London Town's aburnin' down. This is the second time in your life, Mocker, you've ever been known to be right on anything. Take a squint, Captain Mike. The river *is* on fire, or else the world's comin' to an end!"

Mike turned his head and stared hard and long at the approaching specter. His forehead and temples turned red beneath their deep tan.

"Wonder if it could be one o' them newfangled steamboats?" asked the Mocker. "Mebbe Colonel Bisby was right after all."

Mike turned and stared at the long billowing plumes of black smoke growing larger and larger.

"Mocker, you're right for the third time in a row," said Micky, grinning. "Now I know for sure the ol' world's goin' to blow up an' bust!"

As the strange craft approached, Mike's eyes glowed redder and redder. The craft's side wheels were now in plain view, churning up the foam. They heard strange sounds from the exhaust pipe: *pe-we-e, we-pish; pe-we-e, we-pish; pe-we-e, we-pish-sh-sh*. This steamboat was bearing down on them with even greater speed than the *Flying Dutchman*.

"You better ease *Light Foot* over a bit to larboard, Captain Mike," said Carpenter, "and give her a free channel to pass."

Mike gave Carpenter a dirty look, and then pushed the tiller in a bit.

Micky was growing excited. "She's aclankin' an' amoanin' worse'n if the whole world was turned into a tinsmith's clatter."

Curious as a child, the Mocker pointed his finger at the smoke and steam. "Just look at her! She must be smokin' a giant's pipe o' Kentuck tobacker. She's so hot her insides are bunin' up, an' she's ablowin' the scaldin' gases through her nose."

"She's makin' more noise'n a thousand tomcats with their tails all pinched in the doorjamb at once," cackled Micky. "Why, all the seven devils together couldn't stir up such a tumult an' mess o' smoke!"

Suddenly Captain Ogden clanged his signal bell.

Micky gave a start, and then grinned. "Must be them grave robbers by mistake got in the belfry o' St. Paul's."

"Of all the peacock vanity!" exploded the Mocker. "See them gilt letters a mile high across her bow!"

"The *New Orleans!*" sniffed Micky. "This is her all right."

Again their talk was silenced by the clanging bell, and then by the patronizing words of Captain Ogden: "Sorry to chase your keelboat out o' the center current, but you can't expect a floating palace like the *New Orleans* to give way to an oversized canoe."

Mike was as furious as an aroused wildcat. "There's a law o' manners against hogging the river!" he exploded. "If ever I meet you on shore, I'll hit you so hard you won't wake up till middle o' next February! Why, I can outhop, outskip, outjump a hundred such fellers as you. Yes, an' I can lick you within an inch o' your life with one hand tied behind my back!"

Mike was still sputtering when he and his beloved *Light Foot* were completely engulfed in a heavy sea of hot cinders and billowing smoke. And by the time the smoke had cleared, the speeding *New Orleans* was out of hailing distance.

Mike spat the crumbling cinders from his mouth and shook himself in disgust, as if freeing himself from vermin. "I never thought I'd live to suffer such a disgrace as this!" he muttered.

With fiddle tucked under his chin, the Mocker began chanting, "*Pee-we-e, we-pish; pe-we-e, we-pish; pe-we-e, we-pish-*

sh." He was evidently searching for a melody and rhythm to fit the strange new noise.

"Say, they musta had two witches' caldrons on board," said Micky. "By the sound they made, they musta been hitched to some sort o' gristmill."

When Mike had his temper somewhat under control, he added, "Looks to me like that vain Captain Ogden has got ahold of the tail of a clawin', bitin' painter that's spittin' fire. Trouble is, he's not goin' to be able to let go till after he's had his eyes scratched out o' their sockets."

"Say," spoke up Carpenter. "Did you notice the undersize of the deck, cluttered on all sides with machinery?"

Micky laughed outright. "Sure, she was so small that when two crewmen shifted their places to take a look at *Light Foot*, Captain Ogden had to command: 'Trim the boat!'"

"What'll you bet, Micky," asked Mike, finally regaining his composure, "that we don't overtake this haughty *New Orleans* with her keel split wide open on some sawyer, mebbe down around the Devil's Raceground, or long before we reach New Orleans?"

"What odds you offerin'?"

"I'll lay you three to one."

"I'll just take you up on that!" shouted Micky in glee. "Accordin' to all laws o' chance, even you, Captain Mike, can't hope to win every time."

Some weeks later when Mike tied up at New Orleans, Colonel Bisby tried to fill his mind with more wonders that were to be.

"You know as well as I do, Captain Mike," began Bisby with expanding chest, "that traffic on these Inland Waterways is

NEW ORLEANS

Your are a fool

booming beyond anything we even dreamed a dozen years ago. Each new boat that comes plowing her furrow down the channel is bigger and faster than the one that came down yesterday. You must have seen the wonderful new steamship, the *New Orleans* — "

Mike interrupted him with the suddenness of a snapping turtle. "That boat's what I call a dirty Yankee trick!"

"Whatever you call it, there's nothing you and *Light Foot* can do about it. . . . Sorry, Captain, to see you're still living in a deep rut. Don't you know the only difference between a rut and a grave is its length?"

"Trouble with this argument we're in, Bisby," boomed Mike, snapping his teeth, "is it's not gettin' us anywhere. Talk's the cheapest commodity in the world; but it takes a strong back an' plenty o' elbow grease an' courage to pole an' drag a cargo o' freight from here to Pittsburgh."

On the upstream voyage Mike tried to grapple with strange new horizons. He had mastered his own world. He still wore his jaunty red feather, and every keelboatman he met respected his physical prowess. His name was still the toast of the river towns. The trouble was that Colonel Bisby had challenged his mind to a battle with clanking, speeding steamships.

One day Mike grew so restless that he decided to go ashore while *Light Foot* rounded Crawford's Oxbow.

"I'll place Carpenter in charge of navigatin' *Light Foot*," explained Mike. "I'm goin' ashore for a few hours, and have a look for wild game. It's been a month o' Sundays since I've set my tusks in the wishbone of a wild turkey or tore venison from a T-bone steak. I'll board you again when you reach Shake's Landin'."

For the following six hours Mike tramped the virgin forest and the rugged hills. Suddenly he found himself standing on an ancient Indian outlook, atop a timeworn cliff, overlooking the lordly Mississippi.

Mike sucked in his breath. He strained his eyes at the scene before him. From beyond the farthest edge of the horizon the vast stretch of water flowed toward him, and in the opposite direction it faded away toward the distant Gulf of Mexico. Kinking and coiling, it flowed like one of the Mocker's mythical sea serpents. Mike could see four different boats, each a mere chip on the mighty current. He removed his cap, and sat down. He placed Bang All across his knees and gazed in mystical wonder as the Indians had done for centuries.

For the first time Mike realized the vastness of the lordly river. So very long he had been aboard *Light Foot*, with the water lapping and tossing at her stem and stern. Astride the tiller, his range of vision had been narrow, from but a few hundred yards to a few leagues.

For the first time he wondered how long the weathered rocks beneath him had looked down at the mighty river, and how long they would continue to look down. He set his elbows on his knees and his chin in his cupped hands, and for the time he was lost in dreams.

Later his sensitive ear caught the faint sound of a crackling twig, and in an instant his practical mind snapped into sharp focus. His eyes peered past scraggly saplings and through clumps of bushes. He detected the faint flicker of a shadow and a minute later another flicker. There followed a long silence, and then he heard a distinct low cluck. Mike puckered his lips, cracked his tongue against the roof of his mouth in an answering cluck. With Bang All primed and ready, he sat as still and silent as the stone beneath him. Ten or fifteen minutes passed in complete silence, and then a gobbler gave his challenging call. Mike waited a few minutes, and then answered with one more low, vibrating cluck. This proved too much for the cautious gobbler, and after another long pause he came on the run, his neck outstretched, looking in every direction. When he reached the spot where he thought the turkey hen must be waiting, he stopped short. His head and throat turned a rich scarlet, and each separate feather came alive, radiating a glowing silvery sheen.

When the gobbler strutted proudly from behind a clump of blackberry briars and into an open runway, Mike crooked his trigger finger. The lordly bird leaped high in the air, and fell to earth. Mike watched the color fade from his head and neck, and the exultant life from his glorious plumage.

Mike threw the slain bird across his shoulder, and started down the steep hillside. Soon he came to the fringe of deep virgin forest of oak and poplar, sycamore and elm, maple and beech and ash. Instinctively his body reverted to the poise and wriggling movement of his Stone Age ancestors stalking game. He had seen deer signs. Moving forward with easy caution, silent as a shadow, he backed up against a great sycamore tree, and stood there without moving a muscle.

After a long wait Mike caught the flicker of a distant shadow out of the corner of his eye. The tree was his shield, and he waited patiently. The shadow was waiting, too. Mike wondered if the deer had seen or scented him. Many minutes later the shadow moved in his direction. It moved steadily forward, and Mike scarcely breathed as it came nearer and nearer. The deer was now in plain sight. It trotted, it leaped gracefully over a fallen tree, it stopped and threw up its head and turned its ears forward. It looked and listened, sniffing the breeze. Then it seemed to make up its mind. It came forward at a lively trot.

Mike placed his fingers in the corners of his mouth and blew a shrill blast. The surprised deer stopped short. At the split second when it threw up its head and snorted, Mike bent his trigger finger. With tail and head down, the deer ran fiercely for a hundred yards, and then fell dead. By the time Mike reached the animal, all the innocent wonder and fear had gone from its eyes. Its alert, vibrant body lay limp and still.

Quickly and expertly Mike cleaned the carcass, grasped its front pasterns in one hand and its hind pasterns in the other, and threw the body across his shoulders. He stooped, picked up the turkey in one hand and Bang All in the other, and started toward Shake's Landing.

Mike cached his game behind a log and sat down on the corner of the dock with Bang All across his knees. A few minutes later he looked up to see *Light Foot* rounding the Oxbow. He stood and removed his cap. To his eyes she was the loveliest boat in the world. This was the first time he had ever watched her from shore, and his eyes grew misty.

The long oars moved in perfect rhythm. Astride the tiller stood Carpenter, directing the craft with the poise of a seasoned captain. Everything was moving like clockwork.

As *Light Foot* slid alongside the dock, Micky looked around and thought Mike had returned empty-handed. "What kind o' luck did you have, Captain?"

"Where are your eyes?" answered Mike, returning the banter. "Can't you see anything?"

"We're still lookin' around," drawled the Mocker.

"Well, then, hop ashore, the both o' you," boomed Mike grinning, "and tote this turkey and venison aboard in a hurry."

Carpenter looked on in great admiration while the game was brought aboard. "You are sure a wonder at hunting, too, Captain Mike."

"An' since you're doing all right at the tiller, son, I'll just take care o' this meat before it's flyblowed."

While *Light Foot* moved slowly upstream, Mike skinned the venison and feathered the turkey. He started a fire in the clay box amidships, and salted down and dried a part of the meat.

"You fellows are doin' so well navigatin' *Light Foot* that I may as well throw some victuals together. You know I can hardly wait to set my tusks in a juicy piece o' steak."

When he had the food ready, Mike called to Carpenter to order the anchor out. After the men had eaten their fill, the Mocker chanted. Their faces relaxed and their feelings expanded.

"This isn't such a bad old world after all," said Mike, lounging back against the cargo box. "As long as there's still room for wild turkeys an' deer, there's nothing much for us to worry about. And say, I'll be pocked with fleabites if I didn't see fresh signs o' black b'ar in the deep woods this afternoon. Next trip upstream, we'll all indulge in a bit o' fun. We'll tie *Light Foot* up at Shake's Landing long enough to go ashore an' have a good ol'-fashioned huntin' spree. If there's anything that's better'n venison, it's the caul fat an' liver of b'ar."

12. The Usurping Steamboat

Mike's worry about the large number of river craft grew worse with each voyage.

"If this thing keeps on much longer, there won't be room enough left for a catfish to navigate in. As it is now, I have to keep the tiller bobbin' back an' forth an' *Light Foot* weavin' in an' out like a sea serpent. Every kind o' fool craft you can think of is acrowdin' down the center o' the channel, an' drivin' honest traffic crazy!"

"What would you say, Captain Mike," drawled the Mocker, "if we asked the Government at Washington to widen the O-hi-o-o to the size o' the Massassip an' then make the Massassip the size o' the Gulf o' Mexico?"

"Huh!" sniffed Mike in disgust. "Even then we'd have to be dodgin' fool Yankee craft, an' we'd be forced to one side by usurpin' steamboats! There's no use talkin', Uncle Charley was right. When a place gets so cluttered up you can't endure it any longer, thing to do is pick up your traps an' move West. I've heard tell the ol' Missouri is still wide open to honest traffic. The fur trade out that way is beginning to boom. I hear its call."

To ease the tension, the Mocker tucked his fiddle under his chin, and began to chant one of Davy Crockett's ballads.

> I'd like to have a little farm,
> And leave such scenes as these,
> Where I could live without a care
> Completely at my ease.
> I'd like to have a pleasant house
> Upon a little farm,
> Airy an' cool in summertime,
> In winter close and warm.
>
> If I had these I would not ask
> For anything beside;
> I'd be content thus smoothly through
> The tedious world to glide.
> My little wife an' I could then
> No earthly troubles see;
> Surrounded by our little ones,
> How happy we would be.

The Mocker laid his fiddle across his knees. "Sometimes, Micky, I think Captain Billy, years ago, was pretty smart to leave us when he did."

"He wasn't as dumb as we thought at the time," agreed Micky. "And yet, come to think of it, Cap'n Billy's missed a lot o' good times by not bein' with us."

Micky noticed Mike shift his position at the tiller, rub his eyes and stare hard and long, and then pull his cap forward. Micky looked, and saw a splotch of smoke where the water and sky met.

"Captain Mike," said Micky playfully, "you must be lookin' for that wife ol' Mocker's just been lispin' about."

Mike was completely absorbed, and did not answer.

"Then you must be lookin' for some steamboat," added Micky.

Mike's mind was so intent on what he saw that he didn't even hear what Micky said. His face grew hard as granite, with the wrinkles so deep they seemed to reach to the bone. Slowly his color deepened from a red glow to a lurid purple.

By this time the faint smudge of smoke had grown to a plume. Then the smokestacks could be clearly discerned. Micky became so excited that he forgot his manners.

"Bless my heart," shouted Micky, "if I'm not in the middle of a nightmare! That must be the *Enterprise* we been hearin' so much about. She's already beat us by four weeks. She's now pushin' against death an' high water, back towards Pittsburgh!"

Mike seemed tense as an alert deer. Again he heard not a word.

Aroused to deep feeling, Micky gave Mike a sharp slap across the shoulder. "Captain Mike!" he shouted shrilly as a tin whistle.

Mike slowly turned his eyes, but his mind was still on the advancing steamship. "What you want?"

"Don't you remember that bet you made with me that the *Enterprise* would never pass us on its upstream voyage?"

Mike doubled his fist and took a step forward, for the moment forgetting his sweep. Quick as a frightened tomcat, Micky flew to the stem of the boat. "Another word out o' you," boomed Mike, "an' you'll wake up in the middle o' next January!"

The intense fury in Mike's voice sent a deep shudder through every crewman's heart, and each man knew enough to keep quiet.

The steamship had now approached to within a few hundred yards.

"Man your oars!" roared Mike in deep fury. "Row as you've never rowed before! *Pull. . . . Pull. . . . Pull. . . .*"

A minute later the bell sounded from the steamship, and the deep foggy whistle sent the echoes flying in all directions. "Turn that keelboat to larboard!" shouted Captain Shreve through his cupped hands.

"There's no human or divine law that gives the center of the river current to such bullies as you!" boomed Mike, holding *Light Foot* to her course.

The breast wave from the steamboat almost capsized *Light Foot*. A live cinder landed on Mike's shoulder and burned through to his flesh. He clawed it away like a wildcat. His fury blurred his sight.

Next minute the steamship's paddle-wheel bearing struck *Light Foot*'s prow and split her wide open. A terrific crash followed.

Mike was flung headlong against the side of his cargo box. His yawl was pitched overboard, and floated quickly away in the steamboat's wake. Under her heavy cargo, *Light Foot* was quickly sinking. With instant presence of mind, Mike lashed Bang All across his shoulders. His powder horn in his teeth, he swam rapidly toward shore, head held high like a muskrat's. He heard Captain Shreve order *Light Foot*'s crew rescued.

A few minutes later Mike scrambled up the slippery river-bank, and sank down heavily on a piece of driftwood. Elbows on knees and chin in cupped hands, he stared into empty space, trying to collect his thoughts.

In another minute Micky and the Mocker and Carpenter reached shore, puffing and spouting river water. They clambered up the riverbank, and in bewildered silence sat down beside Mike. The other members of *Light Foot*'s crew were now aboard the *Enterprise*, which at the moment was disappearing around the bend in the river.

A long silence followed. "What next, I wonder . . . ?" Micky murmured to himself.

"What next . . . ?" repeated the Mocker, running his fingers through his matted hair. After another long silence he added, "I don't know as I care, much. . . ."

Still dazed and trying to understand what had happened, Micky asked, "Cap'n Mike! Cap'n Mike, what did you do it for?"

Mike's eyes were still staring into empty space. He was still too deep in his own thoughts to hear Micky's question.

The Mocker's fingers began working as if he were playing a tune. "Only thing botherin' me," he said, giving a long sigh, "is how do you suppose the bull alligator is ever goin' to learn to play my fiddle?"

Micky wriggled to ease himself inside his wet clothes. He heard Mocker's question and grinned. "What you suppose the bull alligator's got all them sawteeth along his spine for?"

[141]

"I fear my fiddle's a total loss," groaned the Mocker. "And 'twas my closest friend!"

"Praise be to the angels for that!" cackled Micky, putting his hand to his left eye, which was beginning to swell shut. "Now, at last, mebbe we'll all be gettin' a minute of peace an' quiet."

"But you're forgettin'," answered the Mocker, a twinkle in his eye, "that I can still whistle an' chant!"

"If you know what's good for you, you won't start any more o' your discord for a long time."

Catching sight of Micky's swollen eye, the Mocker added, "That steamboat captain must 'a' give you a regular haymaker!"

Their nonsense was interrupted by Carpenter's despair. "What are we ever going to do, Captain Mike? We're stranded here in the middle of the endless wilderness — and with nothing to eat!"

"Use your eyes, lad," said Micky. "With the one eye I have open, I can see we still have Bang All and a horn o' dry powder."

The mention of Bang All aroused Mike from his stupor. He put a protecting arm around Carpenter. "Don't worry, son." Mike got up, wriggled his body to free it from the clinging clothes. He looked hard at Micky and the Mocker.

"What you two lookin' so glum for?" he asked pointedly. "When all's said an' done, we're not too bad off. Leastwise, I still got all I had when I started on my first keelboat voyage. Yes, an' come to think of it, I got more than I had then. Besides Bang All and a horn o' dry powder, I got my clothes sewed full o' valuable coins. If I wanted to, I got enough money to buy a dozen keelboats."

Micky and Mike and Carpenter ran their fingers up and down their shirts and trousers to make sure their money was safe.

Micky smiled, and said, "The flirtin' ol' girl sure ditched us in a hurry, an' lured us near to destruction."

"Nonsense!" snorted Mike. "I still love the flirtin' old girl as much as ever. The fault was all mine. For a minute or two I lost my head, that's all."

"You lost more than that," drawled the Mocker. "My fiddle's lost, too!"

"But where are we going to go from here?" asked Carpenter, still in despair. "We surely can't live on mudturtles and wild swan."

"We still got our two good feet under us and our two good eyes to guide us," said Mike in mild reproof. "Keep a stiff upper lip, son, an' I'll lead you out o' this smooth as a greased pig."

Micky grew restless at the delay. "Which way you plannin' to travel?"

"Upstream!" Mike barked. He shrugged and twisted inside his clinging shirt. "I been asked to be the captain of one of the big keelboats up the Missouri. Don't be so upset about things. We still have plenty o' fight left in us. Trapping mountain lions and grizzly bear up in Montana will be child's play compared to what we been through. So cheer up!"

"I never been so happy in my life," said the Mocker with a grin and a shrug.

Soon they were on their way. Mike started off, nimble as a moccasined savage Indian. He set out at a hard pace along an old buffalo trail. Micky followed in high spirits at his heels, while Carpenter strained every muscle to keep in third place.

The Mocker fell into an easy stride, and brought up the rear. Before he was aware, he began whistling an improvised melody that fell in with his loose-jointed gait, and after a while he began chanting:

> First upon the heeltap
> Then upon the toe,
> *Hayfoot, strawfoot,*
> Here we go.

13. Mike Fink's Fame

Mike Fink's setting out for the Missouri and the Far West marked the end of the Keelboat Age on the Ohio and the Mississippi. Civilization had surged forward with ever increasing speed, and had brought with it the Age of the Steamboat.

Mike served his generation faithfully. He did easily what others dared not even try. Everywhere he went, his jaunty red feather — the red feather he wore to show his physical prowess after whipping every strong man up and down the river — fired men's hearts. His humor set them laughing. His physical might met every challenge. Mike's fame is not based on dollars and cents. His personality has become a part of our American heritage.

The rivers still flow. Mike Fink's legendary fame still continues down the years. Almost any day, at any of the river towns, one still meets old storytellers, dreamy-eyed and eloquent, who repeat, over and over again, and with ever greater gusto, tales of Mike Fink's deeds.

Author's Note

My boyhood imagination was kindled at my mother's knee by tales of my grandparents and their trek across the Alleghenies and down the Ohio. After all these years, it has been a distinct pleasure to find the leisure to delve into many diaries and records and retrace the Westward March of early American Civilization. Despite hardship and privation, these forebears carried the flag of their hope high as they fought their way over every obstacle. Today we can take heart from them as we move forward to new and difficult tasks.

My thanks go to those who have placed in my hands the rare and authoritative documents used in filling in the background of this story.

J. C. B.